SHOPERAPY

and the Dubai Dilemma

Stephanie Scott

Copyright © 2025 by Stephanie Scott

All rights reserved. No part of this publication may be reproduced, stored, or transmitted in any form or by any means, electronic, mechanical, photocopying, recording, scanning, or otherwise, without written permission from the publisher. It is illegal to copy this book, post it to a website, or distribute it by any other means without permission.

This novel is entirely a work of fiction. The names, characters, and incidents portrayed in it are the work of the author's imagination. Any resemblance to actual persons, living or dead, events, or localities is entirely coincidental. Stephanie Scott asserts the moral right to be identified as the author of this work.

Stephanie Scott has no responsibility for the persistence or accuracy of URLs for external or third-party Internet Websites referred to in this publication and does not guarantee that any content on such Websites is, or will remain, accurate or appropriate.

Designations used by companies to distinguish their products are often claimed as trademarks. All brand names and product names used in this book and on its cover are trade names, service marks, trademarks, and registered trademarks of their respective owners. The publishers and the book are not associated with any product or vendor mentioned in this book. None of the companies referenced within the book have endorsed the book.

First edition Editing by Sarah Linke

Find out more at reedsy.com

Prologue

Blog:
Posted: 5:52 AM (GMT)
User: Your Fashion Ellie-vator
Subscribers: 483

Good morning you GOOOOOrgeous people! Did you miss me?? I can hardly contain my excitement as I sit here, sipping my coffee and typing away about my recent fabulous holiday! After an incredible time in the sun-kissed paradise of Dubai, I'm back and ready to spill the tea or should that be Champagne? on all things fashion, friendship, and a sprinkle of romance that was oh-so-needed after opening Shoperapy.

For those of you who are new here (hello to my 141 lovely new followers), I am Ellie, the proud owner of Shoperapy, a fashion shop like no other! You don't just buy a new outfit here; oh no, you might just leave with a new friendship, and who knows, maybe even a hot date! Yes, you heard me right. If I had a pound for every couple that met in my shop, I'd have enough for a one-way ticket to Paris! But not all of us are lucky in love. For the record, I've sworn off romance... at least for now. Clearly, the universe is trying to tell me something, but let's be real...who needs a romantic distraction when there are fabulous outfits to curate and friends to nurture?

Speaking of romance, let's chat about my exciting holiday! So, did I bring back "The One" from Dubai? Well, unfortunately, I did not. However, I did bring back a fabulous new friend named Lily! She took a short break from her hectic job in hospitality to explore the delights of Meadowbank and, might I add, the breathtaking scenery of our gorgeous Scotland. We had the most delightful time discovering new spots to grab coffee and take in the best views. And yes, she had me in stitches when she dared to ask if all Scottish men wear kilts! Honestly, does she think we're all just wandering around in our traditional attire like it's a daily uniform? (But hey, she is going to meet a handsome Scotsman or two; fingers crossed!)

When we weren't galivanting around the city, we exchanged fashion tips (of course), showing each other our favourite pieces and how to style them in unique ways. It was truly a blend of cultures, highlighting both the traditional and the modern styles. We would talk for hours about fashion trends and the stories behind them, each anecdote adding richness to our shared experience. Being the shopkeeper I am, I couldn't resist giving her a little makeover with some of my newest arrivals before we headed out and let me tell you… she looked stunning!

Now, I hope you've been looking after yourselves while I was away! Grace has been holding down the fort at Shoperapy, keeping me updated with your fabulous fashion buys and, of course, the latest on your romantic escapades. I was over the moon to hear she's still dating Everett! Oh, what a couple they make! Their relationship has blossomed beautifully, and I think we all feel like proud parents cheering them on from the sidelines. And get this—she sent Tim packing back to Thailand after he popped up at her door trying to charm her back! I must say, it takes courage to stand your ground like that. Good for her, I say—she's got her priorities straight. Last I heard, Tim has now landed in Japan. Good riddance, right? Who needs drama when you can find joy in fashion?

But the biggest news is that Grace has also decided to hop on the career train and has joined Shoperapy part-time! She's diving into the next chapter in Fashion Design at College. GOOOOOO girl! New man, new career, and of course, a new best friend—yes, you guessed it, that's me! It's a whirlwind of excitement over here, and her enthusiasm is infectious, bringing in a wave of creativity. Together, we brainstormed ideas for design concepts featuring Scottish tartan with a contemporary twist, blending our cultures seamlessly.

At Shoperapy, we embrace more than just fashion; it's all about friendship and a little flirtation when the time is right. As you know, my shop is a haven for all things chic, where every piece tells a story and every customer leaves feeling a little more fabulous than when they walked in.

Now, let's get down to the nitty-gritty. I know you're all itching to find out what's hot in the fashion world for this autumn season! Drumroll, please... the colour of the season is chocolate! Yes, you heard me—a rich, delectable chocolate brown is taking over wardrobes everywhere! Picture this: cosy oversized knits, chic ankle boots in a stunning mahogany shade, and delectable handbags that resemble your favourite confectionery treat. It's all about rich texture and warmth, and let me tell you, the vibes are simply chef's kiss!

Layering is essential this season, so don't shy away from combining luscious chocolate hues with other autumnal colours like burnt orange and deep emerald. Think of long cardigans to throw over your outfits, warm scarves wrapped snugly around your neck, and beanies in complementary shades. Pair this chocolate hue with autumnal golds and deep greens, and you will be turning heads faster than a runway model! Trust me; you want to grab everyone's attention. Who knows what adventures await just around the corner?

Looking for some inspiration? I've put together a little mood board at Shoperapy showing you how to incorporate this stunning colour into your wardrobe. Come check it out next time you pop by! I've even had a go at designing a couple of pieces myself, fusing traditional Scottish patterns with modern designs. Exciting times ahead, indeed!

And let's not forget the most important accessory of all: confidence! No outfit is complete without a big dollop of self-love. Wear your chocolate-brown beauties with pride, strut your stuff, and remind everyone that fashion is not just about what you wear but how you feel in it. So, make sure you're feeling fabulous! Whether it's an oversized sweater that makes you feel like you're wrapped in a warm hug or a pair of skinny jeans that give you that 'wow' factor, own it!

Before I sign off, I'd love to hear from you! What are your thoughts on the autumn trends? Have any of you tried the chocolate look yet? How did it make you feel? Share your gorgeous outfits and stories with us at Shoperapy—it's all about empowering each other! Remember, the best fashion choice you can make, is to express who you are and to wear your personality with pride.

As the leaves turn golden and the air grows crisp, let's embrace the beauty of autumn together. Remember, life is too short not to have fun, so get out there, and stay fierce and fabulous! Until next time, you gorgeous fashionistas.

Much love,

Ellie xxx

Mysterious Email from Dubai:

From: A.J.
To: Ellie Edwards
Subject: Passport Found!
Dear Ellie,
You don't know me, but I found your passport in a café in Dubai. I know how important it is, and I'd like to return it to you. If you're still in Dubai, we could meet up, or I can send it back by post if you've already left. Please let me know how you'd like to proceed.
Best,
A.J.

From: Ellie Edwards
To: A.J.
Subject: Re: Passport Found!
Dear Mystery Man from Dubai,
Thank you so much for finding my passport! I can't tell you how much of a hassle it was and everything else that goes with it! I honestly thought my trip would be ruined. I did miss a full day of shopping though! I've rambled on, haven't I? I'm sorry for the wordy email, but your kindness really brightened my day.
Warm regards,
Ellie

From: A.J.
To: Ellie Edwards
Subject: Re: Re: Passport Found!
Ellie,

Stephanie Scott

I would read anything you wrote to me ... I promise! Your email made me smile. There's something about your wit that caught my attention. Looking forward to hearing more.
Take care,
A.J.

And thus begins a new potential love for Ellie...the woman who has given up on love!

CHAPTER 1: Ellie Edwards

Age: 30

Relationship Status: Foresworn against love—again—but that doesn't stop me helping you find *the one*… or at least *the one for right now*.

Opinion of Love: Always loved being in love and sharing life with someone, but since her latest heartbreak has sworn off love for EVER but is looking forward to helping others find the one.

Style: Classic fashion style, often referred to as timeless or traditional style, with elegance, simplicity, and sophistication.

Ellie stepped off the bus in her brand-new pink Adidas trainers, cream flared trousers and blazer combo, matched with her pink Kate Spade crossover bag with gold clip. Her heart was dancing with excitement at the familiar sights of her hometown which she was about to share with her new friend. She had just returned home from a whirlwind vacation in Dubai, excited and bursting with fresh ideas and inspiration for her growing business, Shoperapy. The vibrant city of Dubai had invigorated her, and she couldn't wait to showcase the contemporary brands she had ordered while away. All those trendy finds from the markets and boutiques that seemed to call her name when she passed.

The air was unusually warm for an autumn day, with just a gentle breeze, rustling the leaves of the trees that lined the shops and cafes. Perfect weather for a walking tour, she thought.

As she stood waiting on the tour to begin, Ellie took in the sights and sounds of Meadowbank and felt a warm rush of happiness. She had adored her time in Dubai. It had been everything she hoped for and more but being home felt like how she felt when wearing her favourite outfit.

However, she hadn't come back to Meadowbank alone. Beside her, with a cheerful smile, was Lily, the Hotel Receptionist she had befriended at her hotel. They had bonded over shopping escapades and mutual appreciation for fashion, tasty food and some bubbles. The extravagance of Dubai ignited a spark of friendship that took them both by surprise. Now, it was Lily's turn for a much-needed vacation, and where better than Ellie's hometown.

"You really must show me all the hidden gems of this place!" Lily exclaimed, her eyes sparkling with excitement.

"Oh, I will, which is why I thought a fun tour would be the perfect place to start."

But, as she spotted their guide who would lead them on their tour, her expectations tilted off course slightly. The man stood there grinning, but Ellie couldn't help raising an eyebrow at his outfit: hiking boots, a bright rucksack, and '*I Heart Meadowbank* 'T-shirt, and to top it off, a baseball cap emblazoned with a local sports team.

"Hey there! I'm Teddy, your tour guide for today!" he announced, his voice cheerful and warm.

Ellie thought... *While he might not have won any fashion awards, it was immediately clear that Teddy possessed a charming sense of humour. His easy-going banter made everyone feel at ease.*

As the group gathered round, Ellie linked arms with Lily, excitement buzzing between them as they settled into the tour. However, just then, Chase came sprinting up, a ball of energy and enthusiasm, his face flushed from effort. "Sorry I'm late! I got caught up at the café!" he panted, hair slightly dishevelled, and eyes wide with misplaced excitement.

Ellie grinned, knowing that introducing him to Lily would bring instant chemistry.

"Chase, meet Lily! She's visiting from Dubai!"

Chase cut her off mid-sentence, his gaze shifting completely towards Lily, leaving Ellie momentarily sidelined.

"Hi, I'm Chase! So, have you been enjoying Meadowbank? I bet it's not nearly as exciting as Dubai!"

"Oh, it has its own charm!" Lily replied, her British twang softening the words.

Chase's instant fascination left Ellie shaking her head with bemusement as she tried to pull his focus back to the tour. Teddy was already warming up to the group, sharing enthusiastic anecdotes about the town. But Chase was far too occupied with his new friend to pay much attention, beaming like a child at Christmas.

"Did you see Ryan?" Chase suddenly exclaimed, his eyes sparkling.

"He's the most handsome guy I've ever seen! And he dresses so sharp, like he walked right off a magazine cover!"

Ellie glanced around, bemused by Chase's enthusiasm.

"Chase, focus! You're missing the good bits about Meadowbank's sporting history!"

But her shushing only encouraged his excitement further. As Teddy pointed out a quaint café that had been serving the locals for generations, Chase chattered incessantly about Ryan's swagger, developing a rather overdramatic tale. Each attempt to shush him only made him louder, totally lost in his fantasies.

"Honestly, Ellie, that small interaction we had earlier. He smiled at me as he walked by! That's a sign, don't you think? We're destined to be together!" Chase insisted, throwing his arms into the air with wild optimism.

Meanwhile, as the group moved along, Ellie's attention drifted away from the historical details of Meadowbank. She couldn't shake the feeling that Teddy kept sneaking glances at her, punctuating his words with smirks that set her heart racing.

"Isn't this bridge lovely?" Teddy remarked, gesturing gracefully towards a weathered stone structure with intricate carvings. But during his explanation, he turned to Ellie, flashing a grin.

"We locals like to say it's a romantic spot. Perfect for first dates!"

Ellie felt her cheeks warm as he winked at her, convinced he was trying to flirt. "Oh, is that now, Teddy?" she replied, her voice teasing as she nudged Lily.

As the tour continued, Teddy shared stories about local heroics, guided them to the town's memorial park, and discussed its ornate sculptures. Yet Ellie was less enchanted by the history and more captivated by the way Teddy leaned closer when he spoke to her. It was thrilling and disconcerting, and no matter how hard she tried, she couldn't focus on anything else.

Eventually, when the tour wrapped up and they stood near the edge of the beach gazing out at the frothy waves, Teddy called for Ellie.

"Could I have a word?"

Heart racing, she stepped away from the group. This was it, she thought. She mentally rehearsed a way to let him down gently, preparing an eloquent speech about her unwillingness to engage in romance.

"I just wanted to say…" Teddy began, but Ellie cut him off before he could finish.

"Teddy! I'm flattered, really! You seem like a wonderful person with an amazing sense of humour, but… "…I've kind of sworn off love. It's nothing personal—I've just realised I'm not letting anyone in. So, thank you, but that's a hard pass."

Teddy blinked, his easy-going smile fading into an awkward pause. He scratched his neck with a sheepish grin, leaving Ellie feeling a touch embarrassed. Why must guys keep falling for her?

But then he unexpectedly replied, "Sorry, but I actually wasn't interested in you."

Ellie stared at him, mouth agape. "Oh?"

"Yeah, I was interested in your friend." He nodded over her shoulder.

Turning, Ellie caught sight of Lily, who was now blushing crimson. In that moment, Ellie's heart sank and laughter bubbled inside her. Could it really be that her friend, just steps away, was the centre of Teddy's affection?

Trying to recover from her string of embarrassment, Ellie chuckled. "Of course! What I meant to say was I'm your exclusive wing woman today."

"Oh, good, good," Teddy replied with a relieved smile.

As she agreed to pass on her friend's number, a flurry of adrenaline surged through Ellie, blending embarrassment with a surprising wave of satisfaction. Her heart still thudded from the misunderstanding, but she couldn't help smiling at the absurdity of it all. She felt a pang of delight for Lily's unexpected fortune, but her own heart still thudded from the earlier confrontation. Arranging their number exchange, she made a note to check in with Lily later to relive the curious turn of events, but for now, all she could do was laugh at the peculiarities of her own romantic misadventure.

As they wandered back to the town square, the autumn sun basked everything in a warm glow, and laughter bounced through the winding streets of Meadowbank like leaves fluttering in the crisp breeze.

From: A.J.
To: Ellie Edwards
Subject: Hello again!
Hey Ellie,
How is your day today? I thought I'd drop you a message because I've been thinking about you today.
I was in town earlier and saw the cutest café! I thought to myself... Ellie would like that café!
Enjoy the rest of your day/week.
Cheers,
A.J.

From: Ellie Edwards
To: A.J.
Subject: Re: Hello again!
Hi A.J.,
I'm having an enjoyable day so far. What about you? That café sounds intriguing! I'm always up for pastries and a good chat.
Pity I am not in Dubai!
Talk soon!
Ellie

CHAPTER 2: Sara Buchanan

Age: 23
Relationship Status: It's complicated! In a relationship with a much older man and fallen head over heels.
Opinion of Love: Believes age is just a number.
Style: Girly, feminine fashion. Likes maxi dresses, skirts, shirts, and lots of fabulous colours, but lately, has been hiding in leggings and sweatshirts while at university. Now no longer a student is looking forward to wearing some of the new feminine fashion trends.

Sara paced nervously in front of the shop entrance, her heart racing with a mix of dread and inexplicable anticipation. The sign above read 'Shoperapy,' glowing cheerfully against the grey backdrop of the Scottish sky. Her mum, Victoria, had been raving about this shop for weeks, painting vivid pictures of soft fabrics and stunning styles. Yet here she was, trying to muster even a flicker of excitement as she prepared to step inside.

"Sara, come on! We've got to get you a new outfit," Victoria called, already striding towards the door with a confidence that only a parent could possess. Her enthusiasm was contagious—or at least, it should have been.

 The truth, however, was that Sara wished the celebration of her recent graduation could involve absolutely anything else.

"Can't we do something different? How about a nice lunch? A girls' spa day?" she offered, her voice faltering beneath Victoria's resolute smile.

A subtle shake of her head was enough to dispel any notions of relaxing massages or leisurely brunches. Victoria had evidently decided that for her daughter's journey into adulthood, there had to be a new wardrobe.

"No, no, no. You have to meet Ellie! Plus, I really want you to let me get you an outfit for your beautiful newly graduated life! Just think about how lovely it will be!"

Victoria replied, making it nearly impossible for Sara to protest any further. What was it about parental enthusiasm that struck fear into young hearts?

Sara huffed as they stepped through the threshold. If she were to be honest without fear of reprisal she possessed an alarming lack of direction regarding her future. What did one wear in their newly graduated life?

I don't really know.

Surely leggings and an oversized hoodie weren't suitable for the occasion.

As the door chimed and the smell of new fabric enveloped her, Sara felt herself soften slightly. The shop was exactly as lovely as Victoria had promised, adorned with pastel hues, and delicately arranged racks that seemed to echo the promise of style and sophistication. Small displays of accessories added a whimsical charm. Ellie stood nearby, unfazed, and friendly, a warm smile stretching across her face. Next to her was Grace, the new shop assistant, who stood eagerly, notepad poised, ready to take notes on style and fabric.

"Oh, Sara! So lovely to meet you!"

Ellie exclaimed, bending slightly to form an intimate circle, as if sharing a delightful secret. "Your mum has told me so much about you!"

Sara felt her stomach clench. Why was she suddenly the centre of all this excitement? Unable to ignore the sinking feeling, she attempted to deflect the attention.

"Um, it's nice to meet you too! Just, uh… curious about what you've got in stock."

"Let's get started, yeah?" Victoria cut in, a gesture towards the racks making it all too real.

"I mean, what I wear really doesn't" but her mum flooded the conversation with endless suggestions, mirroring rather than soothing Sara's uncertainty.

"Try this on! It'll look amazing!"

Victoria persisted, sparking a flurry of activity around her.

"Actually, I don't think purple's really my colour…"

Sara mumbled, the familiar itch of frustration rising in her throat. "And that scratchy fabric doesn't suit me at all…" Her attempts at diplomacy only incited further enthusiasm from her mother, who waved her concerns aside with casual dismissal. Desperation tugged at her as the minutes stretched on, feeling like hours. It wasn't that the clothes weren't beautiful, nor that Ellie and Grace weren't utterly charming. But the expectation loomed heavy upon her shoulders like the thickest of clouds, and Sara felt the need to reveal her biggest secret kept too close to the chest.

"Ellie, can I talk to you for a second?" Sara whispered to her, stealing a glance at her mother who seemed completely absorbed in a vibrant red dress.

Leaning in, she whispered,

"I'm almost five months pregnant… and my mum doesn't know."

Ellie's eyes widened, instantly on her side.

"Oh goodness! That explains a lot!" she said, eyes sparkling with both empathy and excitement. Grace nodded vigorously, leaning in with quiet, encouraging murmurs.

"Listen, we can definitely help you with this. Don't worry first up, we need to find some styles that'll keep your bump hidden!" Ellie said, her expression firm with resolve.

Motivated by their new goal, the three women browsed the clothing racks together, looking for fashionable yet roomier outfits that would help conceal Sara's sensitive situation. The camaraderie blossomed as Grace chimed in with her opinion, tossing around style terminology that made Sara feel, for once, like a fashionista.

Just as they began to compile a small array of beautifully flowing tops and clever layering strategies, Victoria's voice rose from the other end of the shop…

"Oh Sara, darling, let's try this!" She wielded a figure-hugging dress, bright blue and sparkly, as if graduation attire required sparkle.

Sara swallowed hard, her heart sinking.

"No, Mum, not that. I mean, I don't think."

"Oh no, sweetie," Ellie jumped in smoothly, "This trend is all about showing off your figure! You've got such an amazing silhouette!"

"But that's just it," Sara interjected, panic rising in her chest.

"I've got a… situation I need to manage here."

Ellie masked Sara's secret with a smile warm enough to melt ice.

"Let's just play it cool. The flared and oversized styles are the way to go! They're in vogue right now, so chic!"

Sara watched as they spun their fabric web around Victoria, who remained blissfully unaware of the tension unfolding. In their expert hands, the loose blouse swayed gently with every movement, when Charlie's name flashed on her phone screen, causing her to clutch it desperately.

"Mum, can you let me take this?" she called across the shop, but Victoria was too wrapped up in trying to find the perfect style for her daughter to notice her urgency.

"If it's Charlie, just tell him you're busy!" Victoria called out, blissfully oblivious to the mental juggling act her daughter was performing.

Sara bit her lip, glancing nervously at Ellie and Grace. They exchanged knowing looks, giving a thumbs-up in silent solidarity.
She pressed decline, but the phone vibrated insistently, a reminder of the outside world she was simultaneously excited and terrified of entering. Finally managing a quick breath, she decided to focus on the warmth of companionship around her rather than the weight of her own doubts.

The rest of the shopping session transformed as fabrics twirled around and Grace and Ellie found her a splendid ensemble… that evoked a blend of elegance and ease. Their laughter mingled with the whirl of excitement and Sara found herself relenting, swept up in it all.

"Yes, these baggy trousers are definitely the trend!" Grace cheered, holding them up enthusiastically.

"Let's avoid revealing too much," Sara blurted, rebellion stirring inside her as they all merrily conspired.

"You'll thank us later," Ellie said with a wink as the gaggle of women revelled in their secret adventure a perfect mix of hilarity and shared connection that pulled them closer together.

The world outside beckoned, but within these carefully curated walls of Shoperapy, Sara finally felt a flicker of joy blossom, intertwining with fear in a tender tapestry of newfound excitement. One thing was for sure—the path ahead held surprises she hadn't anticipated, but at least she'd have the right clothes to face them.

Charlie? Why is Charlie calling you?'

Charlie was her father's best friend a man who had always treated her like a little girl. Why would he be calling her now?

Sara played it off and distracted Victoria with the 'perfect' pair of shoes for her and thankfully it worked.

Sara escaped Shoperapy with her secrets intact, *for now,* but she'd never known shopping could be so stressful.

CHAPTER 3: Lily Javed

Age: 28

Relationship Status: Single and too busy to even consider love.

Opinion of Love: Too busy working to think about it but loves observing relationships at the hotel.

Style: Hotel uniform, navy suit, cream blouse, and red and cream scarf. Think all outfits should be accessorized with a cute silk scarf.

Lily twirled in front of the mirror, admiring the delicate lines of the dress she wore, a unique piece from Shoperapy that felt like a second skin, hugging her curves effortlessly. The fabric flowed elegantly as she moved, accentuating her slender frame and giving her an air of confidence that she hadn't felt in ages. Beside her, Ellie was equally entranced, her ensemble gleaming with extravagant accessories sourced from Dubai's bustling markets. The two women, with their laughter echoing off the walls like music from a beloved song, were a perfect combination: Lily, the city girl who'd immersed herself in the luxurious world of hotel life, and Ellie, the adventurous spirit who'd sought out hidden gems in every corner of the globe.

As they prepared for the evening, the air was filled with excitement, punctuated by the sound of clinking glasses in the background and the faint notes of a guitar that floated in from a nearby cafe. Their evening commenced in a quaint local restaurant that Ellie had insisted on visiting, a stark contrast to the grand hotels where they often dined. The little eatery was tucked away down a cobbled street, adorned with fairy lights that glimmered like stars, casting a soft glow around their table and illuminating Lily's face with a warmth that made her forget her earlier apprehensions.

"This place is magical!"

Lily exclaimed, her eyes sparkling with delight as she glanced around, taking in the rustic decor, the aroma of spices wafting through the air, a sensory invitation that drew her deeper into the experience.

Yet, a pang of guilt nudged at her heart as she sank into her chair. When they had been in Dubai, Lily had continuously taken Ellie to the same five-star hotel restaurant, dominated by opulent decor and an atmosphere that, while luxurious, left something to be desired in terms of authenticity. For all its dazzling highs, Lily realised it couldn't compare to the soul of the local dining culture she was now immersed in. The food was exquisite, undoubtedly dazzling with international finesse and presented like art on a plate. But somewhere in her, a desire had sparked to discover local culture, which had taken a back seat to the safer choice of the hotel's grand dining.

How could she have deprived Ellie of so many culinary experiences, the kind that weaved stories into every bite? Their menus were filled with delightful items Lily couldn't pronounce, and as they placed their orders, her apprehensions began to ease. The waiter, with a warm smile, recommended the house special a fragrant dish brimming with spices and fresh herbs that overwhelmed Lily's senses in the best way possible. As they settled into comfortable conversation, the initial enchantment of the restaurant slowly waned, giving way to a more pressing topic. Ellie leaned in, her face alight with mischief and a twinkle in her eye that promised trouble.

"So, what about Teddy, our charming tour guide?"

The mention of Teddy sent a blush flooding to Lily's cheeks, an involuntary reaction that Ellie noticed immediately, raising an eyebrow in amusement. Truth be told, Lily had been tiptoeing around the subject, weary of the implications that loomed over her like a thick fog. She let out a nervous chuckle, trying to shift the topic like a leaf caught in an unpredictable breeze, hoping to steer the conversation into calmer waters.

"Oh, you know… he was a nice guy, but…"

"Lily,"

Ellie interrupted, her tone serious yet playfully teasing.

"We are going to talk about this whether you like it or not!"

Another sigh escaped Lily's lips, laced with both frustration and affection.

"What's the point, really? My life isn't here."

The weight of her words hung in the air, heavy with resignation. it was a truth she was still coming to terms with.

Ellie rolled her eyes dramatically, wafting a hand as if to dispel Lily's concerns.

"That's no reason not to have some fun! Teddy's charming, he knows the cool places around town, and who knows, maybe he'll introduce you to something profound."

Her enthusiasm was infectious, and Lily found herself wavering.

"But it's not like I'm going to drop everything I have in Dubai and move across the world!"

Lily protested, her voice a mixture of disbelief and hope an admission of what, deep down, she secretly wished could happen.

The idea of leaving the comforts of the familiar played on her mind like a lingering note of a song she couldn't quite catch.

Ellie smiled knowingly, her eyes sparkling with determination.

"You don't need to drop everything right away, you know. Just dive into the moment. Life isn't all about practical decisions!" She pointed at Lily while taking a sip of her richly brewed coffee, her expression earnest and vibrant. "We can just enjoy ourselves! You deserve a little fun after all that hard work at the hotel."

Lily's heart raced as they moved on to dessert an enchanting concoction that made her momentarily forget the earlier conversation. The sweet smells enveloped her; a comforting embrace of chocolate and vanilla that made her eyes widen with delight. Yet excitement and sadness clashed within her, leading to a battle of conflicting emotions she hadn't anticipated.

"Let's think outside the box here." Ellie gestured animatedly. Her voice rich with excitement as she launched into a string of humorous suggestions to convince Lily to call Teddy.

"Imagine us trying on dresses and booking restaurants, and Teddy getting us discounts!"

Lily laughed despite herself, envisioning their escapade in a whirlwind of excitement and losing herself momentarily in what could be. But still, hesitation lingered, jostling her thoughts like bustling crowds, each doubt fighting for attention.

Feeling finally encouraged as the last forkful of dessert melted away, a mixture of resolve and fear solidified in her chest.

"Alright, let's do this."

Ellie clapped her hands with joy as they left the restaurant. The evening air blooming with possibility.

"Now, let's head to Shoperapy to get you all glammed up!"

Ellie's excitement was unmistakable, enhancing Lily's spirits as they stepped out into the vibrant night.

As they wandered along the cobbled streets, the faint sounds of laughter and music filled the air, each note adding to the evening's magic. Ellie's playful nudging stirred Lily's anticipation, her mind a swirl of what-ifs and dreams. She pulled out her phone, her finger hovering over Teddy's number, her stomach fluttering with nerves.

"Okay, but you need to choose my outfit!"

Lily exclaimed, looking back at Ellie who grinned from ear to ear, her excitement almost tangible.

"Oh, I wouldn't have it any other way!"

Ellie bounced on her heels, embodying the spirit of adventure she was trying to coax out of Lily.

Lily hesitated, biting her lip as she pressed the call button, half-expecting a reason to hang up. But before she could lose her resolve, Teddy answered, his voice enthusiastic and bright, the sound of laughter in the background mingling with his greeting.

"Lily! I've been waiting for your call!"

His excitement washed over her like a warm wave, melting the earlier tension that had gripped her. Ellie stood by her side, practically bouncing on her toes as they waited to hear what Teddy had planned, her enthusiasm igniting Lily's courage.

Suddenly, Lily felt alive, as if she were stepping into a vibrant movie scene she'd only ever imagined, her heartbeat syncing with the thrill of the unknown.

Teddy launched into a whirlwind of suggestions: dancing beneath the stars, visiting local art galleries, trying out the newest food places in town, all of it delivered with such charm that Lily couldn't help but nod along, captivated.

"I've thought of all the places we could go! There's this fantastic hidden spot where they do jazz on Thursdays, and I just know you'll love the vibe!"

His words wrapped around Lily's heart, and she couldn't help but smile, realising how much she had longed for experiences like this, filled with wonder and spontaneity, a stark contrast to her meticulously scheduled life back in Dubai.

As their call wrapped up, Lily felt a sense of giddiness she had nearly forgotten. After she hung up, Ellie grabbed her hand and nearly dragged her towards Shoperapy, her eyes gleaming with the promise of excitement.

"We need to prepare for what's ahead! Dresses, shoes, bags—it's a whole new world waiting for you!" she declared, practically squealing with joy.

Lily took one last look back at the charming restaurant, marvelling at how in a few short hours her world had shifted dramatically. It was as if she had walked out of her life as mere employee, bound by expectations, and stepped into a vibrant tapestry of opportunity and new experiences. For the first time in ages, she wasn't bound by concerns of practicality or set plans. She felt an awakening within her, softly coaxing her to embrace the unknown.

As they stepped into Shoperapy, she felt the flicker of hope blossom within her, hinting that this might be a turning point, a step into a new chapter filled with delightful surprises.

But the pair stopped dead in their tracks outside the store.

Someone had vandalized the entire storefront and the surrounding shops, with spray paint. It was a colourful, intricate design one Ellie might have appreciated if it hadn't been splashed across her shop window surrounding the words:

Do you know your neighbour?

CHAPTER 4: Ellie

Ellie stood in front of the large windows of Shoperapy, her heart racing with a mix of excitement and anxiety. Her lips tugged into a determined smile, trying to keep her spirits high despite the unsightly splashes of colourful paint sprayed across the glass. "Just a minor hiccup," she muttered to herself, squaring her shoulders. Today was the Autumn Open House. Only two hours remained before guests arrived to celebrate the turning season. The idea of transforming Shoperapy into a warm, inviting space filled with autumn cheer spurred her on, despite the graffiti mess that threatened to overshadow her hard work.

"Grace!" she called out, her voice bright and cheerful as she rushed towards her friend, who was carefully arranging an array of festive treats on the long wooden table. The scents of spiced chai and an assortment of fall cookies pumpkin spice, apple cinnamon, even a batch of crunchy pecan tarts wafted through the shop like a warm embrace, mingling with the crisp autumn breeze that filtered through the door as it swung open and shut.

"Oh, Ellie! Just in time!" Grace replied, her face lighting up as she hurriedly pointed to a pile of ornamental garlands. "Can you help me hang these garlands? They're meant to create the perfect autumn atmosphere!" Ellie could hardly contain her enthusiasm as she clasped the garlands in her hands, vivid bursts of colour in shades of red, orange, and gold. "Of course! Let's make this place magical!" she exclaimed, her excitement bubbling over.

As Ellie climbed the ladder to drape the decorations with careful precision, her mind raced with thoughts of what today could hold. She hoped that the Open House would not only be a celebration of seasonal change, but a moment of connection for people in the community, all seeking to embrace new beginnings. "A new season, a fresh start," she thought to herself with optimism sparkling in her heart.

Just then, her gaze landed on a figure ascending the sidewalk. The window cleaner had finally arrived, carrying a sturdy ladder and a bucket of soapy water at his side. He looked over at Ellie and gave a small wave, his smile almost illuminating the autumn day. As she stepped into the cheerful sunshine to greet him, she couldn't help but admire how handsome he was. Dark hair framed his face, and warm blue eyes sparkled with an easy charm.

"Hello there! I'm Noah," he said, his easy smile making her heart skip.

"Hi, I'm Ellie. Thanks for coming on such short notice," she replied, her cheeks heating slightly in the sun and the moment. Perhaps it was the ray of sunshine that was brighter suddenly, or maybe it was Noah's infectious smile that made the day feel even warmer. A hint of flirtation danced through her mind, but she quickly dismissed it. Love was something she had decided, quite ardently, to put aside for now.

Noah chuckled as he began to clean the windows, his motions deliberate and confident.

"Ah, you must be excited for the big event. **Autumn Open House**, right?" He leaned back slightly, wiping his brow with exaggerated flair, and Ellie couldn't help but grin at his theatrics.

"Absolutely! We're hoping it'll be a wonderful way for everyone to embrace the new season," she beamed, taking a moment to watch him work. There was a playful, almost teasing glimmer in his expression that made her pause, as though he knew the power of his charm.

Just as she was about to ask him whether he might fancy a cup of chai before he started washing the windows, a sharp, brisk voice cut through the air.

"Excuse me." A woman in a severe black suit marched up to them, her sharp heels clicking against the pavement, instantly commanding attention.

Ellie couldn't help but feel that this woman was anything but festive, with an air of seriousness that dimmed the joyous atmosphere.

"Can I help you?" Ellie asked, forcing a smile despite her instincts telling her that this newcomer was not there to join in on the festivities.

"I'm Amy," the woman replied, adjusting her glasses with a precision that suggested she wielded them like a shield.

"I've been invited to some… autumnal shopping thing by my little brother's girlfriend?" Her voice wavered slightly, filling the air with a sense of uncertainty about why she had come at all.

Ellie's heart raced. "Oh! The Open House isn't for another hour and a half, but you're welcome to join us early! We have lovely chai tea and cookies!" The offer tumbled out, sincere enthusiasm spilling from her lips as she gestured towards the inviting table laden with tempting delights.

Amy's expression remained fixed, resistance evident in the way she crossed her arms defensively.

"That sounds great, but… I'm not really looking to socialise," she replied, her tone stiff and weary, as if the mere idea was intolerable.

"More cookies for me, then." Ellie joked, trying to lighten the atmosphere, but the stiff woman merely raised an eyebrow, signalling her lack of interest in Ellie's cheerful spirit. Meanwhile, Noah clearly lavished his attention on Amy, who didn't appreciate the attention.

"So, what do you do, Amy?" Noah ventured, flashing his enigmatic grin as he reached for his cloth to polish the glass. Ellie watched curiously, wondering if Amy would respond. She sensed the tension between them growing, like thick fog in the cool autumn air.

"Marketing," she said bluntly, her expression unchanged, much like a sentinel guarding against any attempt at camaraderie. "And you?"

A cloud of flirtation hung heavily between them, thick with unmistakable awkwardness. Ellie shifted nervously, trying to ignore the frustration crackling in the air around the trio. Just then, Noah laughed, leaning even closer to Amy, a playful tone infusing his words as he attempted to charm her.

"Great! I bet you know all about mixing styles in your work!" Noah quipped, tilting his head slightly as if searching her expression for any hint of warmth.

Strangely enough, Amy only huffed in response, her eyes narrowing, seemingly annoyed rather than intrigued. "Not really my thing."

Ellie felt a wave of empathy for both parties: Noah, desperately trying to connect; Amy, resolutely refusing to budge. And yet, Ellie knew from experience that love often creeps in under the most bizarre of circumstances.

The tension continued to build, and Ellie shuffled nervously in place, hoping that the ice could somehow thaw. Then, as if the universe was playing a cruel trick, Noah laughed again and leaned even closer, enthusiasm spilling over.

"You see, I usually just focus on cleaning windows," he said, his tone light-hearted as he continued polishing. He flashed another winning smile, confident and warm.

But then, disaster struck. In that very moment, as he reached over to switch his cleaning bucket to a better angle, the unexpected happened. The bucket tipped precariously over the edge, and Ellie's breath caught in her throat as the murky water cascaded quickly downwards. In a dizzying flash, before Ellie could even shout a warning, it splashed over Amy, soaking her from head to toe.

A thick silence enveloped them like a heavy fog. Ellie's cheeks burned with humiliation as she gaped at the absurdity unfolding before her. Amy stood frozen, her mouth slightly agape, as the shock washed over her like the torrent of water that just drenched her. Strands of her hair were plastered to her face, and her pristine black suit was now an oversized sponge, dripping with grimy water.

"I'm so, so sorry!" Noah exclaimed, his eyes wide as saucers, dripping with sincere horror at what had just unfolded.

"I didn't mean to!"

"Obviously!" Amy snapped, shaking droplets from her coat and her voice dripping with irritation, her cheeks flushed with rage as she stared incredulously at Noah.

"Well, I suppose this is one unconventional approach to breaking the ice!" Ellie chimed in, desperation lacing her humour, but it fell flat against the heavy tension in the air.

"Are you alright?" Noah asked, stepping closer, concern and bemusement mingling as he eyed the mess he had just created.

It was clear that Amy was both mortified and furious, but Ellie sensed a crack in her steely exterior as frustration began to give way to sheer disbelief about what had just happened.

Amy's lips twitched, and for a fleeting moment, Ellie thought she might burst into laughter, perhaps out of sheer disbelief rather than mirth. Instead, she took a deep breath, letting it out slowly.

"No, I am not alright! You just covered me in dirty water!" She fumed, her voice a mix of exasperation and indignation.

Ellie stepped in, hoping to calm the storm brewing between them.

"How about I get you a towel?" she suggested, desperate to salvage what was left of the day.

"And maybe another cookie?"

Amy's eyes flitted to her, and Ellie could almost physically feel the tension begin to thaw, just a touch.

"I would need a whole box of cookies to be alright again," she grumbled, but Ellie could see there was now a faint twitch of amusement lurking just below the surface, threatening to rise.

"No problem, I'll fetch a whole supply!" Ellie offered, a glimmer of hope flickering within her.

"And I promise to personally make sure you are ready for the evening."

With renewed determination, Ellie dashed inside, determined to make this day as memorable as it was chaotic. She pulled out fresh towels, golden cookies, and a big jug of warm chai tea. She could hear laughter coming from outside, a mixture of Noah's charming repartee and Amy's reluctant chuckles as the ice melted away between them.

When she returned, she found Noah, still standing awkwardly, while Amy was now attempting to dry her hair with the towel Ellie had provided.

"You know, this gives new meaning to 'making a splash' at an event," Noah joked, and Amy struck a half-amused, half-annoyed look, finally cracking a smile as she tossed the towel aside.

The atmosphere had shifted dramatically, and Ellie felt a swell of pride as she watched the tension dissipate before her eyes. Ellie's heart beat with renewed joy, maybe this *Autumn Open House* wasn't going to be the picture-perfect celebration she had envisioned, but it was turning into something far more memorable. There was a distinct warmth blossoming among them, laughter echoing through the windows and mixing with the golden light of the streetlamps outside.

As they continued to joke and tease, creating an unexpected camaraderie, Ellie resolved to embrace whatever came next. The mishaps, the surprises, and the laughter, were all part of the beautiful tapestry of life and friendship that blossomed amidst the chaos.

With thoughts of forgiveness, humour, and a sprinkle of magic in her heart, Ellie knew that today would be a story worth telling, even with the bumps along the way. After all, that was the spirit of community, love, and celebrating life's little messes together.

She'd seen some rocky starts to love, but this might be the rockiest ever.

Finally, Amy, in a tense voice, asked Ellie:

'Might you have anything in your store that is simple and black?'

Ellie squirmed; she was mildly allergic to the words *simple* and *black*.

Definitely not," she said brightly, "but I *can* find you something far more glam.

CHAPTER 5: Amy Carter

Age: 37

Relationship Status: Single

Opinion of Love: Not interested. Love only causes misery. Happier to be on her own… or is she?

Style: Fashion, what's that? Black is her favourite colour to wear and the simpler the better.

Amy stood at the entrance of Shoperapy, bracing herself for the chaos awaiting her inside. The delightful boutique was basked in warm hues of golden autumn, the rich scent of freshly baked scones wafting through the air, mingling with the chatter of excited shoppers. To Amy, who avoided crowds like the plague, the space was absolutely packed. She felt a wave of anxiety wash over her as she took a moment to gather her courage.

"What on earth were you thinking, Adam?" she muttered under her breath, spotting her brother across the room, enthusing over a display of colourful scarves lining the walls like a burst of confetti. Feeling her stomach churn, Amy couldn't shake the sense of dread building within her.

As the fashionistas filtered in, she caught sight of Jess, Adam's new girlfriend, surrounded by a gaggle of well-wishers, all of them laughing and chatting excitedly about the event.

Unsure why she had agreed to this whole 'Open House' shindig, she vividly recalled the moment Adam had insisted,

"Please, just give it a shot with Jess. She's lovely!"

Sighing, she shifted uneasily in a ruffled dress bursting with vibrant patterns, very different from her usual comfortable jeans and oversize hoodies. The garish attire felt like a costume, as if she were trapped in a role she never auditioned for.

"What was I thinking?" she grumbled, wishing fervently she was wearing her own clothes, not some colourful outfit styled by Ellie.

Yet, the hopeful glimmer in Adam's eyes had left her with little choice. She adored her baby brother, but this felt like an extravagant waste of her time and energy.

With a quick glance around, the shock of the bucket of water crashing over her earlier shimmered in her mind like a neon sign. The memory was a warning siren blaring away in her thoughts, signalling that she absolutely should have stayed home, tucked up on the couch with an enjoyable book and her beloved cat.

"Amy! Oh, you look fabulous!" Jess squealed, her voice cutting through the cacophony. Amy plastered on a dry smile, feeling the heat of discomfort rise in her cheeks. Each compliment felt like a well-placed jab to her self-esteem, rather than the sincere praise it was meant to be. No amount of flattery could mask the awkwardness blooming inside her.

"What a stunning, vibrant dress! It really suits you," Jess continued, her zest seemingly boundless.

"Yes, it's something," Amy replied, forcing herself to maintain eye contact. She noticed that Jess was already surrounded by her own entourage of friends, all of whom gushed over her. Why couldn't they all just leave her alone? Just beyond them, she caught Adam peeking through a rack, delivering a thumbs-up as if this moment were an Olympic event. Understandably, he wanted them to bond over something — but things just weren't working for her.

"Are you enjoying the party? I mean, isn't it delightful?" Jess chirped, pulling Amy deeper into the throng of guests. The buzz of music surrounded them, yet Amy could only feel the weight of the crowd pressing in on her.

"Delightful," Amy echoed, casting a quick glance at her watch. What she really wanted was to escape the cheerful clutches of the upbeat crowd—to snuggle into her old, dog-eared fantasy novel and forget all about impending social obligations. The notion of encountering more people and forcing herself to make small talk made her even tenser. She really needed some air.

"Oh look, they've got cupcakes!" Jess exclaimed, steering Amy towards the dessert table adorned with the most colourful confections. Amy's heart plummeted. Tales of engagements and wedding preparations weren't on her table of delights tonight.

"Come on Jess, can we just go grab a drink?" Amy asked, her voice thin, barely rising above the excited calls of the crowd.

"What? You don't want to eat? It's all part of the experience!" Jess replied, oblivious to Amy's increasingly desperate attempts to escape the celebration. Each word grew more cheerful, placing additional weight on Amy's nerves. Why couldn't anyone decipher her reluctance?

"Seriously, a drink will do me good right about now," Amy insisted, attempting to pull gently on Jess's arm towards the bar. But there was something in Jess's eyes those bright, eager eyes that brought Amy's resolve crumbling down. "To be fair, Adam has never had a serious relationship before," Amy reminded herself.

This playful distraction in winning over Jess likely wouldn't last long anyway.

As she turned to gather her courage for this ridiculous social venture, Ellie swooped in unexpectedly, her hair a glittery halo against the gentle lighting of Shoperapy. "Amy!" Ellie beamed, her crystal glass filled with sparkling champagne practically radiating positivity. "How come you didn't tell me that Jess was engaged?! You called her your brother's girlfriend, and I had to learn from Victoria that she's, his fiancée!"

In that moment, time seemed to slow down, and the room felt like it was spinning. The colour drained from Jess's face, leaving her pale, a stark contrast to the vibrant party surrounding them. "Engaged?" Amy spluttered, her mind racing as her eyes darted from Ellie back to Jess, confused by the sudden revelation. How could Jess be engaged? They had only started dating recently a matter of weeks ago! She felt foolish for not digging deeper into their relationship sooner.

Ellie, finally noticing the shift in atmosphere, stopped her animated movements her champagne glass hovering in midair, the fizzing bubbles dancing away like Amy's mounting panic. She quickly turned to Jess, failing to read the distress washing over her.

"Jess… you're engaged… to whom?" Amy asked, her tone edged with incredulity and annoyance.

As Jess hesitated, Amy's heart raced each second felt heavy, a palpable silence creeping over them despite the buzz of celebration in the background. She felt the room closing in around her, a swirl of abstract conversations blending into a chaotic symphony, friendly laughter reduced to a distant hum beneath her rising anxiety.

"What in the world have I walked into?" she thought bitterly.

The mention of 'engagement' turned her stomach into knots like poorly tied ribbons. Jess opened her mouth as if to speak, but no words emerged. She cast a quick, anxious look towards Adam, who was now blissfully engaged in a conversation about plaid shirts with another guest, blissfully unaware of the drama unfolding around him.

"Jess?" Amy pressed, unwilling to let this slip by without understanding what was really happening.

When Ellie sensed that something was up, she stopped celebrating, her champagne glass undrunk in her hand.

Amy looked at Jess. "You're engaged… to whom?"

Jess was sheepish as she answered in the now-deadly quiet shop: "Surprise…"

A tentative smile broke across her face, albeit with a hint of uncertainty.

"Actually, I was going to tell you today. It just happened so quickly!" she blurted out, her words rushed, carrying an earnestness Amy wasn't sure how to respond to.

"Oh, I'm sure it did," Amy replied, feeling irritation seep into her voice. "You only started dating my brother, what two weeks ago?"

"Exactly! But we have this amazing connection! Don't you see it?" Jess exclaimed, her enthusiasm faltering slightly under the weight of Amy's scepticism.

"Jess, I" Amy began again, struggling for the right words to ease the tension in the air and respond to Jess's hopeful gaze, which now sought acceptance. Just then, Ellie, sensing an opening, broke in with her characteristic energy.

"Oh, Amy!" Ellie chimed in, "Don't be all negative and sceptical!" Love's an adventure! Just look at how sweet they are together!" she emphasized, gesturing towards Adam and Jess, whose laughter rang like music around the room, buoying the atmosphere.,.

She surveyed the daunting spectacle of happy faces… celebrating something fun and light-hearted while she was trapped inside a tornado of foul thoughts and an internal monologue that refused to quiet. She wanted to escape, but

Adam's gleeful attitude made her heart ache. The jovial comments continued to roll through her mind, like a soundtrack she could not turn off.

"Adventure? More like a train wreck waiting to happen,"

Amy mused silently. her arms crossing defiantly over her chest.

Forcing herself to hold her tongue, Amy turned to gauge Jess's response, looking for signs of sincerity. Amy's brows furrowed, demanding clarity. Despite her brother's optimism, she could not shake the feeling that this could end disastrously. Shaking her head, she searched for an escape route, longing for the tranquillity that awaited her back at home with her favourite novel.

Attempting to make her stealthy exit, she passed a group of chatty women, industriously discussing the latest trends in autumn fashion and the glamorous wedding plans unfolding like a new chapter. The chatter wove through her mind like tangled threads, further draining her spirit. "Excuse me, could I just…?" she began, but the interruption was swift as Ellie bounded up once more, gripping her arm like a lifeline.

"Wait! Everybody, let's raise a glass to Jess and Adam!" Ellie proclaimed loudly, her voice dominating the rest of the crowd, a dazzling grin plastered across her face.

Ellie knew she had to do the right thing for Jess, no matter how Amy was feeling, and Amy knew that was her cue to disappear. She couldn't bear to stay amidst the festivity and noise any longer. As she plotted her retreat, however, she heard Jess call her name aloud with urgency.

"Amy! Wait!"

It was the underlying desperation in Jess's voice that halted Amy in her tracks, compelling her to turn back and face the burgeoning crowd. She caught Jess's pleading gaze, those hopeful eyes reflecting everything: the night's sparkle, the excitement, and a hint of fear for the future.

"Please, just give it time, okay? I promise, no pressure," Jess pleaded softly, her sincerity rendering Amy's heart a little less guarded just enough to quell her initial instincts. Perhaps this bizarre evening could turn into something unanticipated, something quite unlike the gloomy aftermath she had envisioned.

In that moment, Amy, feeling a tug at her heartstrings, nodded slowly, opening herself to the possibility that she could learn to understand Jess's story. It was going to be a long night, which was certain, but just maybe Amy could find a way to build some sort of friendship with Jess.

CHAPTER 6: Sara

Sara stood frozen in the middle of Shoperapy, her heart racing as the silence enveloped her. Just moments before, laughter and light-hearted chatter had filled the air, intertwined with catchy beats that had made everyone tap their feet in time. Bright lights glimmered from the displays, and the irresistible smell of fresh coffee wafted through the shop, mingling with the sweet scent of freshly baked pastries. There was a sense of community and warmth as the patrons enjoyed each other's company, sharing stories and laughter. But now, with the sudden halt of the background music, a heavy atmosphere replaced the jovial buzz. All eyes were firmly trained on Ellie and the two unfamiliar women standing nearby, an uncomfortable tension gripping the room.

Her mother leaned closer.

"That's Jess," she pointed subtly, the one getting married. The other woman is Amy, Adam's sister. She just met Jess today and had no clue about the engagement."

A wave of embarrassment washed over Sara as she realised how awkward the moment had become, a palpable tension that seemed to coil tightly in the air, as heavy as a blanket. It felt as if a thick fog had descended upon Shoperapy, muffling the vibrancy of the earlier camaraderie and allowing uncertainty to creep in like an unwelcome intruder.

Glancing at Amy, Sara could see the confusion etched on her face, her brows knitted in disbelief, and Sara's heart twisted for her. Hurt flickered in Amy's eyes; the sudden nature of the revelation felt like a cruel twist of fate, turning what should be a joyful occasion into an evening of discomfort. Jess, on the other hand, looked as though she was lost in her own discomfort, shifting from foot to foot while casting anxious glances at Amy, equally trapped in the turmoil of unexpected emotions. There should have been excitement, congratulations a celebration of love and promise. Instead, an overshadowing sense of unease loomed like dark storm clouds threatening to burst, amplifying the silence that had taken hold of the shop. A stark contrast to the happiness that had filled the space just moments earlier.

The seconds stretched into what felt like an eternity. The silence was almost deafening, the tension so thick it felt tangible, wrapping around everyone like a vice. How long could this dreadful pause last, stretching the boundaries of comfort beyond recognition? Sara's mind raced with possible scenarios, each more outlandish than the last: perhaps the two women would laugh, perhaps there might be tears, or maybe they would leave in anger. Those moments resided in the realm of uncertainty, where reality felt surreal, as if they were trapped in a bubble waiting to either burst or break free. It was time to break the spell, to shatter the awkwardness that had gripped the shop and its bewildered patrons. Somehow, she had to reclaim the cheerful spirit that had filled the space only moments ago and dispel the heavy silence weighing down on them.

Sara took a steadying breath, her heart pounding like a drum in her chest, almost drowning out the cacophony of thoughts racing through her mind. This was not just about Jess and Amy anymore; this was about her too. Her mother was bound to find out about her news eventually, particularly with the way her belly seemed to grow by the day. The timing could not have been better, not with the weight of this secret firmly planted on her shoulders, a heavy weight of apprehension sitting on her conscience. She couldn't keep it hidden any longer; it had burdened her for too long, and if Jess could handle that level of surprise, then perhaps she could handle the shock of her own while transforming the room from dread into something beautiful.

With tentative but determined steps, the click of her heels magnified against the floor. Sara made her way to the centre of the shop, drawing everyone's gaze. Every step felt like a mile, heavy with expectation. She cleared her throat, the swell of anxiety shifting into resolve.

"Excuse me, everyone!" Her voice rang out, gaining strength as she continued. The room fell eerily quiet; every pair of eyes fixed on her.

"I have an announcement to make."

Faces shifted eyes widening, brows lifting anticipation rippling through the crowd like a held breath.

"I'm... pregnant."

The words spilled from her lips like confetti, and for a moment, time froze. Then a collective gasp swept through the shop, voices blending into a murmur of shock and disbelief. Victoria stood rooted to the spot, mouth slightly agape, eyes wide. The colour drained from her face before rushing back tenfold, emotion flickering wildly as she tried to process what she had just heard.

"Pregnant... but when?" she managed, her voice unsteadies, surprise forcing her onto autopilot.

"I mean how? I know how, but ..." Her words tumbled out in a flurry, an endearing mix of confusion and excitement that drew a ripple of soft laughter from the crowd.

Sara chuckled gently, the absurdity of the moment breaking the tension, exactly as she planned.

"I know, Mum. It's a lot, but"

Relief washed over her as Victoria's shock gave way to total happiness, her emotions swinging between disbelief and elation.

"But my darling," Victoria said, her voice trembling, "I'm ecstatic!"

And with that, Sara was engulfed in the tight embrace of her mother, who was warm and full of happiness, a fierce protective love radiating from her like a protective, loving mum. Tears brimmed in her eyes as she drew back slightly, placing her hands on Sara's swollen belly, the reality settling deeper with every heartbeat.

"Oh, look at you," she whispered. "My little girl is going to be a mum."

The celebration that followed felt like a breath of fresh air. Laughter erupted once more, the joy returning to Shoperapy as though it had never left.

Jess approached cautiously, her face lighting up with a relieved smile, surprise softened by understanding.

"Congratulations, Sara. And… thank you for bringing some light into this moment," she said warmly. Bridging the gap created by the earlier awkwardness, allowing everyone to breathe again. Sara returned her smile with a wink, a quiet reassurance that the earlier discomfort was fading, replaced by warmth once again.

"Don't worry," Sara added softly. "Amy will come around. She'll see how wonderful this engagement is."

Sara promised Jess, her heart swelling with hope, a glimmer of optimism piercing through the lingering tension.

As the friends began to mingle, laughter and chatter filling the space, Shoperapy transformed back into its sanctuary of happiness.

Victoria returned, eyes sparkling.

"I couldn't be happier, darling. You're going to be an amazing mum."

As her heart swelled with pride, Sara felt lighter than she had in days, her burdens falling away like autumn leaves. Here, amid the chatter and camaraderie, her secret had become a shared moment of happiness.

Victoria wagged a playful finger at her.

"But no more secrets, right?"

Sara smiled and promised, watching her mother walk away content.

But she knew it wasn't true.

There was another secret she was keeping.

And this one might be far harder for her mother to swallow than a baby.

She had shared only half the truth and somehow, she felt even more on edge than before.

Ellie to Jess: Jess, I am so sorry about revealing your secret, I was just so excited to hear the big news from Victoria. I had no idea it was a secret!
J to E: Oh Ellie, it's okay. It's just that Amy is so against me and Adam. I don't know why, but she doesn't like me.
E to J: I'm so sorry and that can't be right. Everyone loves you, Jess. You are so lovely…
J to E: Aw, thank you Ellie. That means a lot. xxx

CHAPTER 7: Lily

Lily was used to blending into the wallpaper. As a junior receptionist at a hotel in the centre of Dubai Marina, her days were typically smooth and quiet, marked by a sea of nameless faces. With her crisp uniform and neat bun, she was both part of the establishment and entirely invisible. A polite smile and nod sufficed for the odd guest or two, but beyond that, her name might as well have been *Vacancy*.

Yet there was one person who made her feel seen: Teddy.

Teddy was the spirited tour guide who could turn the mundane into magic. With tousled brown hair and an infectious smile, he had a knack for whisking Lily away from her grey routine, suggesting adventures through quaint streets and breathtaking views. They were just getting settled on this escapade and today was supposed to be a grand tour or at least, that's what Lily had thought.

"Lily, I need you to know," Teddy said conspiratorially, flashing his trademark cheeky grin,

"I'm about to divulge some of my hottest secrets. Places so special they're not in any tourist brochure. These are just for you and me."

His eyes sparkled with mischief as he leaned closer, sending a flutter of excitement through Lily's chest. A whirlwind of emotions followed. Who would have thought a handsome tour guide could make her feel so special? In her navy uniform and name tag, she often felt like a ghost drifting through the hotel halls but with Teddy, she felt like a vibrant star stepping into the spotlight.

"You know," Lily started, letting her laughter linger in the air, "my uniform never really lets me stand out."

The sea breeze filled her lungs, fresh and invigorating. She twirled slightly, the floral dress she had carefully chosen with Ellie swirling around her legs, making her feel light and alive.

"In fact, I think I'd be mistaken for a lamppost sometimes!"

For a brief moment, there was silence then their shared laughter echoed warmly around them.

Teddy laughed, the sound bouncing off the nearby monoblock.

"Well, if you're a lamppost, that makes me a perfectly cheeky squirrel. And I'm just here to lighten things up. You are far too beautiful to fade into the background."

He winked, and Lily felt her cheeks warm with a blend of embarrassment and delight. Everything seemed bathed in sunlight, an almost cinematic glow surrounding them.

When Teddy slipped his fingers between hers, a jolt of exhilaration rushed through her. Together, they ambled down the street on their adventure. As they walked, Teddy amused her with anecdotes and snippets of trivia, his passion for the town and its quirky history bringing colour to moments she would have once thought dull.

"I know this sounds a bit odd," he said, eyebrows waggling mischievously, "but wouldn't it be wonderful if buildings could talk? Imagine the gossip they'd have: 'Does the old bakery still make those legendary scones?' Or 'Did you hear what happened at the butchers last Tuesday? Absolute scandal!"

His whimsical tone made Lily giggle, and she found herself picturing animated buildings gossiping like old friends, their brick façades brimming with stories just waiting to be told.

She was finally beginning to understand how much passion Teddy poured into his work. It was infectious. His enthusiasm swept her along, and simply being near him made her world a little brighter.

Just then, something in the distance caught Lily's eye, drawing her attention away from Teddy. A delicate little shop nestled behind fragrant lavender bushes beckoned her closer. An intricately painted wooden sign flapped cheerfully, announcing:

Silk Printing Studio

The place looked charming and inviting, small, snug, and full of promise. It whispered of creativity and artistry, of quiet afternoons spent making something beautiful. The scent of lavender mingled with a faint hint of dye, drifting through the air and tugging at her curiosity.

"I've always loved silk scarves," Lily said softly, glancing at Teddy, whose eyes mirrored the spark lighting her own.

"I see so many women at the hotel wearing beautifully printed silk scarves, but they're always so expensive. I've often thought about designing my own... if I ever had the time, or the courage," she added with a small laugh.

The thought lingered as she gazed through the shop window, dreams of silk and colour slipping through her fingers like sand through an hourglass. Finally, she turned back to Teddy with a polite smile, ready to move on and continue their spontaneous day.

But Teddy had other plans.

"Hold your horses, Miss Lily!" he exclaimed dramatically, stopping so suddenly she nearly bumped into him.

"We are *not* walking past a silk printing studio," he declared. "This is an excellent opportunity. We absolutely must go in."

His eyes twinkled as he flashed her a wide, encouraging grin, igniting a flicker of hope deep within her.

"Wait what about the tour?" Lily asked, glancing between him and the enticing little shop, excitement tangling with nerves.

"You had places to show me. Are we really stopping here?"

The familiar fear of stepping outside her comfort zone crept in, intertwining with the thrill of possibility.

Teddy placed a hand theatrically on his chest and adopted a mock-serious tone, reminding her vaguely of a famous actor mid-monologue.

"Lily, my dear, my tour can wait. This town has been here forever, and it isn't going anywhere. But a moment like this when curiosity taps you on the shoulder? Those don't wait around. Miss them, and they're gone."

His sincerity struck something deep inside her, sparking a quiet courage she hadn't realised she was carrying.

"So… you really think we should go in?" she asked, her voice wavering between doubt and excitement.

Teddy nodded enthusiastically, his smile lighting up his entire face.

"If you're even slightly interested, I'm not letting you leave until we explore this little gem."

"Who knows? This could be the start of something. Your passion project. Something that's just for you."

His exuberance was contagious, and Lily found herself unable to resist as a wave of determination washed over her.

"Alright then!" she squeaked, her resolve strengthening as they approached the door. Her excitement built with every step, echoing the rapid heartbeat racing in her chest.

As they entered the studio, the soft scent of lavender blended with the rich aroma of dye and fabric, surrounded them in a soothing embrace. It felt like stepping into another world, one infused with artistry and warmth. The walls were adorned with vibrant silk samples, each a small masterpiece, highlighting colours so vivid they seemed to leap from the fabric. Intricate patterns and delicate designs danced across the silks, each fold whispering a story of creativity.

The owner, an elderly woman with twinkling eyes and hands stained with colour hands that spoke of years devoted to her craft, greeted them warmly.

"Welcome! Are you here to try your hand at silk printing?" she asked. "It's a delightful process. There's truly nothing like it."

Her melodic voice instantly put Lily at ease, replacing the stiffness she often felt back in the hotel lobby, with a surprising sense of belonging.

Lily's heart raced, excitement and apprehension tangling together. The idea of trying something new thrilled and terrified her in equal measure. Teddy stood beside her, radiating encouragement, his confidence spilling over and lending her strength. He gave her a thumbs-up.

She hesitated for only a moment, her natural shyness bubbling up then she straightened.

"I'd love to try," she said boldly, surprising even herself as courage surged through her.

"Brilliant!" Teddy cheered, clapping his hands together.

"I knew you had it in you, my artistic lamppost! Look at you sparkling already."

His words warmed her, pushing aside the doubts that so often whispered in her mind.

As the studio buzzed gently around her, Lily imagined herself creating beautiful silk scarves pieces that hotel guests might admire, maybe even treasure. The thought filled her with a soft, glowing pride. Perhaps today wasn't just a casual outing with Teddy. Perhaps it was the beginning of something unexpected, something entirely her own.

Just as she gathered herself, Teddy grabbed a brush and brandished it in mock combat.

"Fear not, my budding artist!" he boomed dramatically. "I shall be your valiant knight, defending you from the dragon of self-doubt!"

The owner and another customer chuckled, and Lily burst into laughter, her nerves evaporating like mist in the sun.

In that moment, her insecurities loosened their grip. Laughter stitched a deeper connection between her and Teddy, illuminating the room from the inside out. Beneath the humour and playful theatrics, something warm and genuine was taking root.

Underneath all the giggles and jovial antics, the warmth of connection with Teddy blossomed stronger than Lily ever expected. Teddy had an extraordinary way of awakening curiosity within her, unlocking doors she hadn't dared to open. While the world often saw her as a uniform and a name tag, Teddy saw her potential. He reflected it back to her like a mirror, allowing her to glimpse who she could become.

For the first time in a long while, Lily felt ready to explore herself fully to let her sparkle show. This adventure felt like the first brushstroke on a blank canvas, her life waiting to be filled with colour and possibility. feeling like a painter about to fill a blank canvas with all the hues of her newfound enthusiasm, ready to create a masterpiece out of her life.

As they stepped back outside, Lily's gaze drifted down to the park. She froze stunned.

Sara was sitting on a bench near the shore with a man.

An older man. A much older Man!

And they were kissing.

Lily blinked, then smiled to herself. *Good for Sara.*

"Oh, looks like Charlie has found a new romance, and she looks younger than him… much younger." Teddy exclaimed happily.

They both waved over, but when Sara noticed them, she stiffened. A flicker of panic crossed her face before she returned a timid wave and hurriedly pulled the man away.

Lily frowned slightly.

It was odd but mostly, she felt happy that Sara had found someone.

Still… Why hadn't she mentioned it that night at Shoperapy?

CHAPTER 8: Amy

Amy was on her way to meet Jess for coffee, a task she found somewhere between mildly inconvenient and outrageously obnoxious. Dressed in her perfectly tailored suit, a reflection of her dedication to sharp lines and a standard silhouette, she felt as though she were slipping into her work uniform. Even though this particular day was meant to be a holiday from her demanding job in marketing, she couldn't quite shake the professional air that clung to her. It was as if her suits were a second skin, one she had put on long before ever considering the possibility of friendship or a leisurely coffee break.

Her mind drifted back to the long rant she'd endured from Adam after the debacle the other day. He had been laden with apologies for not informing her of Jess's engagement sooner, his disappointed expression more theatrical than she ever thought necessary.

"You were supposed to congratulate her, Amy!" he'd exclaimed, his tone reminiscent of a disappointed fan at a rugby game.

She didn't see why Adam expected her to throw confetti and cheer like an exuberant five-year-old at a birthday party simply because he had found a new love to parade around.

In truth, it stung a little. The idea of protecting loved ones from making mistakes in love was clearly lost on Adam. She could still remember the lesson life had taught her when Matthew had thrown her under the proverbial bus to claw his way ahead in law school. Love, she had learned, was nothing more than leverage masquerading as a fairy tale. It paraded around in pleasing outfits for a while, promising roses, and romantic dinners, until the mask slipped and the true nature of affection revealed itself. So, while Jess might seem nice enough, Amy was convinced she would eventually find a way to hurt Adam. That, she was certain of.

And yet, because Jess was soon to be her sister-in-law, Adam had grown increasingly adamant that Amy found a way to be "friends" with the woman he was going to marry.

A part of her wished Adam understood that the loyalty she felt towards her work and her career far outweighed the shallow exchanges demanded by the world of social niceties. The thought repulsed her; workaholics simply were not designed to *do* friends. Hence, the coffee invitation. The pressure to set aside her cynicism clashed violently with her weary resolve.

As she strode purposefully through the bustling town, each step echoing with her desire to escape the inevitable small talk that awaited her, a bright display of flowers caught her eye, if only for a moment.

"Beautiful flowers, but no time for distractions," she muttered.

Then, amid the crowded stalls, someone called her name.

Naturally, she ignored it, assuming it was another Amy. Honestly, how many Amys could there be?

She turned sharply and found herself face-to-face with none other than Noah, the window cleaner who had found it amusing to dump dirty water all over her just days earlier, a particularly unfortunate incident in her otherwise immaculate life.

"Hello again," Amy said briskly, attempting to free herself from his grip, only to discover that the man was very persistent.

To her dismay, Noah, wearing a grin that hovered somewhere between charming and infuriating, stepped directly into her path, blocking her escape.

The audacity. Amy thought annoyingly to herself.

What did he want now? A repeat performance of his accidental dousing of her immaculate designer suit?

"Hey! I've just come from Shoperapy," he exclaimed, as if that explained everything in the universe. "The vandal struck again!"

His earnest expression suggested he genuinely believed this was riveting news. For Amy, however, it meant absolutely nothing; all she could think about was escaping this conversation as quickly as possible.

Amy nodded, disinterested.

"Fascinating. Well… bye then," she said, attempting a strategic exit, only to find her path blocked once more.

Clearly, Noah hadn't received the memo that she was not available for engaging conversation.

"Wait up! I'm sorry about ruining your clothes the other day," he said, following her like an overly enthusiastic puppy, an image that only irritated her further. Was he truly still trying to charm his way into her attention?

He gestured helplessly, his charm offensive now in full swing.

"Can I make it up to you? How about dinner?" he suggested, flashing an infuriatingly disarming smile, as though proposing a peace treaty after a well-fought battle.

"Absolutely not," Amy replied without breaking stride, her tone a sharp mix of exasperation and disbelief. She was not about to entertain dinner with a man who had recently baptised her designer suit in water and debris that looked like it belonged in a swamp.

Undeterred, Noah quickened his pace to match hers.

"C'mon, are you telling me you've never thought about a little fun? You obviously work too hard. Everyone deserves a break!"

His incredulous tone almost made her crack a smile. His relentless banter grated on her nerves, yet beneath the irritation, there was an unfamiliar flutter deep inside her an unwelcome reminder of emotions she had carefully buried beneath layers of professionalism and cynicism. How irritating it was to *feel* something. To be drawn in by his ridiculous flirtation. How dare he stir feelings that were best left forgotten?

As they reached the flower stalls, Amy noticed Noah beginning to sneeze dramatically, his face contorting in a way that was undeniably amusing.

Ah ha! She thought. There was her one opportunity! Without missing a beat and barely acknowledging how theatrically exaggerated his sneezes had become, she ducked into the nearby flower market before he could catch up. With a flick of her hair, she disappeared.

Inside, fragrant blooms surrounded her, enveloping her in sweetness as her thoughts swirled like petals in a freshly shaken bouquet. Still, a faint sense of panic crept in. Ever since Matthew, she had built walls thicker than any suit could provide. She needed to stay firm. No feelings.

As she wandered between the flowers, Amy smirked at the absurdity of it all.

"Perfect distraction," she murmured, admiring an arrangement of peonies soft pink petals stark against her black suit.

"If I can just figure out how to outwit him…"

That was when she spotted a particularly vibrant cotton-candy-pink arrangement. It reminded her of something she'd once seen on a cheerful television programme, something that screamed happiness frozen in time. Instead of spiralling into her own manufactured despair, she snapped a quick photo, reminding herself that one day of accidental flirtation, did not qualify as life-altering chaos.

Then, from the entrance, she heard the voice.

"Amy!"

Shoperapy and the Dubai Dilemma

Damn it. He'd found her.

"So sneaky!" Noah exclaimed, raising his hands in mock surrender, wheezing slightly from his earlier sneezing fit.

"Do you need a tissue?" she shot back, trying and failing to mask her amusement.

"Funny thing is," he said, recovering quickly, "I was actually going to ask for your number so I could pay you back for your dry cleaning." He winked, clearly impressed with himself.

"Not happening." Her expression stayed deadpan, though inwardly she winced. Maintaining her resolve was getting harder. This banter was beginning to feel like a game one she wasn't prepared to play.

"Two cups of Matchas, then," he persisted, leaning casually against the flower stall like someone auditioning for a romantic comedy.

"I hear it's what all the cool kids drink these days."

"Have you ever considered that *you* might be one of those cool kids looking for trouble?" she countered, a wry smile tugging at her lips.

Noah waved dismissively.

"Me? Trouble? Never. Besides, isn't it your turn to play nice?"

It was a cheeky plea that made her raise an eyebrow

The audacity made her raise an eyebrow.

So, there they stood in an arena of flowers and ironic flirtation. Amy felt irritation flare again, tangled tightly with intrigue. What was it about this infuriatingly charming man that made her feel both annoyed and curious? She shook her head, as if physically banishing the thought. What on earth was she meant to do with *that*?

"Look, you've caused enough havoc for one day, don't you think?" she said sharply, hoping it might distract from the flutter stirring in her stomach.

But Noah only grinned, his enthusiasm annoyingly contagious.

"Just give me a chance."

With that, Amy stifled a laugh.

Maybe a little chaos wouldn't kill her.

Still… getting entangled in emotions had never been the plan.

After a moment of rapid internal calculation, she glanced around and gestured pointedly to the flowers behind her… a sudden idea.

"How about this?" she offered with unexpected spontaneity. "Help me pick out flowers for Jess as token of friendship. Then we're even."

Noah's face lit up.

"You drive a hard bargain. I'm in!"

And just like that, her day off transformed into something frantic yet strangely entertaining. Side by side, they debated colours and meanings, bantering like old acquaintances, turning an ordinary day into something unexpectedly exhilarating.

As they stood together, selecting the final arrangement, Amy felt a quiet, surprising satisfaction bloom.

Perhaps a little chaos, and some fun, was exactly what she needed after all.

CHAPTER 9: Ellie

Ellie stood before the imposing doors of City Hall, taking a steadying breath as her heart raced. She was a small business owner, yes but today, she was more than that. Today, she was a fighter for her little corner of town. The recent spate of spray-paint vandalism had hit her shop particularly hard, leaving her feeling exposed and unsettled. Determined to represent her interests, she recalled the late nights spent scrubbing paint from her windows and the defeat that had washed over her each time, knowing her hard work was being undermined by senseless acts. Each memory fuelled her resolve.

She wore her best cream blazer, hoping it conveyed seriousness despite its whimsical floral pattern. It felt like she was walking a fine line between professionalism and her natural exuberance. In the pit of her stomach, nerves fluttered like trapped butterflies, making her wonder whether she was stepping into an arena where her fierce passion for her shop would be judged rather than understood.

"Just be yourself," she whispered, glancing at her reflection in the glass doors. Her colourful ensemble conservative by her standards still felt like an audacious statement amid the muted tones of the other attendees.

"Well, if they want boring, they can look elsewhere," she muttered, adjusting her collar with a cheeky grin only she could see.

Buoyed by a fresh wave of confidence, Ellie pushed through the doors. The cool air inside wrapped around her like a familiar embrace, invigorating her spirit as she stepped into the bustling world of fellow business owners.

Inside, the atmosphere buzzed with conversation a medley of discussions about business, health, and the unfortunate plight they all shared. Cameron, the local gym owner, stood tall with his arms folded, a posture Ellie knew all too well. It often led to their usual debates, filled with brash yet flirtatious disagreements.

Sighing at the thought of previous sparring sessions where friendly rivalry had sometimes grown a little too spirited, and resulted in a date or two, she decided to stay away from Cameron today.

Instead, she spotted Ryan, the handsome manager of the high-end fashion store across the street. He'd recently caught Chase's attention with his smooth charm and easy smile. Allowing herself a moment of levity amid the seriousness of the day, Ellie took a seat beside him, keenly aware of how striking his presence was.

Chase is smitten, isn't he? she thought with a soft chuckle, but the moment dissolved when her phone buzzed in her pocket, snapping her back to reality.

"Let's get started, shall we?" the councillor announced from the front of the room.

The buzz faded into an expectant hush. Ellie shifted in her seat, her heart pounding as she prepared to hear about the issues plaguing her community. It was easy to feel small in a room full of established voices, but she was determined to make herself heard.

As the meeting began, Ellie couldn't resist glancing at her phone. It had become a lifeline bringing sparks of excitement amid the weight of her business responsibilities at Shoperapy. Yes, it was from him!

The mystery man from Dubai, who had entered her life like an unexpected splash of colour in an otherwise predictable routine. A thrill rippled through her at the thought of A.J. What was he thinking? The anticipation of a reply sent her heart into a dizzying flutter.

While the councillor droned on about policies and proposals, Ellie's mind drifted. She imagined A.J. stepping into her world, serious negotiations interrupted by spontaneous dance-offs in her shop.

"I bet he has some killer moves," she thought, a mischievous grin forming on her lips.

She nearly laughed aloud, quickly stifling it when she caught the councillor's eye. He appeared to be glaring in her direction, clearly unimpressed by her distraction.

"Now, are there any questions?" the councillor asked, scanning the room expectantly.

Ellie's heart raced once more. This was it her moment. The words bubbled up inside her, fizzing and urgent, like a shaken soda can. Drawing in a deep breath, she raised her hand.

"Erm, yes," she began, her voice shaky but sincere.

"I'd really like to discuss the importance of supporting local businesses in tackling the vandalism issue. It's not just paint it's our livelihoods. Every store has stories and dreams behind it, and the community needs to be reminded of that."

The room fell silent.

In that moment, a wave of courage washed over her. A delightful surprise for someone who so often felt overwhelmed by the weight of responsibility.

The councillor nodded, seemingly taken aback by her courage.

"Thank you, Ellie. That's a strong point. Local businesses do bring character to our town."

His words wrapped around her like warmth, igniting her determination even further.

Feeling energised by the small victory, Ellie leaned back in her chair, a smile spreading as she realised, she had taken a meaningful step towards change. The discussion continued, and she found herself leaning slightly towards Ryan, the light-hearted banter between them impossible to ignore.

"Do you think I made a good impression?" she whispered, her tone hovering between humour and nervous hope.

Ryan gave her an encouraging nod, the corners of his mouth lifting slightly.

"More than good, Ellie. You've got spirit. Besides, who doesn't love a bit of flair and surprise amid all this seriousness?"

His compliment sent a pleasant warmth through her, settling just beneath her ribs.

Just then, her phone buzzed again, breaking her momentary reverie. Her heart raced as she glanced down, spotting an email notification from A.J. A thrill surged through her, and she stifled another grin, feeling as though the world had suddenly burst back into vibrant colour.

As the meeting continued, Ellie couldn't help sneaking glances at her phone. She stole a quick look.

From: A.J.
To: Ellie Edwards
Subject: Thinking of you
Hey Ellie, just had some fantastic falafel. Wish you could taste it too! What's happening back in Scotland?

Ellie chuckled under her breath, the grim faces around her blurring into a backdrop of muted tones. If only they knew she was nurturing a budding romance by email with a man thousands of miles away over falafel of all things. The absurdity of it made her smile, instantly making the meeting feel less daunting.

"Right, so we need to discuss ways to curb the vandalism. What do we think? Barriers or nightly watches?" The councillor continued, but Ellie's attention drifted as she typed a quick reply.

From: Ellie Edwards
To: A.J.
Subject: Thinking of you
Oh, I'd love some falafel right about now! Not much happening here, except a grumpy councillor and lots of spray paint!
Ellie

"Anyone have any suggestions?" the councillor asked, cutting through her daydream.

"More lights!" someone shouted from the back, earning a handful of half-hearted nods.

"Ooh, more lights! I love that idea!" Ellie exclaimed impulsively, causing several heads to snap in her direction.

The councillor cleared his throat, eyeing her with faint irritation, clearly surprised by her sudden enthusiasm.

"Er... well, if we're adding lights, we'd need more funding," he began, his tone suggesting her eagerness wasn't entirely welcome. Ellie sensed the crowd's mild disapproval ripple outward.

Ignoring it, a surge of determination bubbled up inside her.

"What about community vigilance?" she added quickly.

"A volunteer night watch with friends and neighbours might work... perhaps?"

Her heart raced as she sent another message to A.J., convinced he'd find the idea brilliant. There was something deeply empowering about being proactive for her community.

From: Ellie Edwards
To: A.J.
Subject: Thinking of you
We're now setting up neighbourhood night watches.
Ellie

From: A.J.
To: Ellie Edwards
Subject: Thinking of you
Night watches? Sounds suspiciously romantic! Count me in!
A.J.

Ellie nearly snorted at his cheeky response. But as irresistibly charming as A.J. was, she couldn't ignore Ryan leaning closer, his brow furrowing with curiosity.

"Hey, you alright?" he asked, concern laced with amusement.

"Yeah, just... erm... dealing with my life decisions," she joked, waving a hand dismissively.

"You know, like saving my business from spray-paint doom."

"Oh, sure. Small potatoes," Ryan said with a chuckle. "Anything else on your mind?"

"Not really," she replied with an innocent smile. "Just keeping up with a faraway friend."

Still, her thoughts spun wildly as new messages from A.J. poured in, forming a delightful secret she carried close to her chest.

Another email pinged, and her breath caught.

From: A.J.
To: Ellie Edwards
Subject: Thinking of you
I'd love to meet up one day. How does London sound?

Before she could stop herself, Ellie was fully pulled back into her digital world. London. With A.J. Her imagination sprinted ahead strolling through Covent Garden, sipping coffee in a quaint café, his laughter mingling with city sounds.

Meanwhile, the meeting droned on, funding debates, damage reports, half-hearted initiatives. Ellie listened with half an ear, smiling to herself as visions of pastries, prosecco, and long conversations danced through her thoughts like butterflies.

"Ellie, you still with us?" Ryan's voice cut through the haze.

She cast her eyes back to him, momentarily disoriented.

"Oh! Absolutely," she said quickly, though her grin betrayed her. The affection bubbling inside her was impossible to contain.

"Well, I can see why Chase is friends with you. He never stops talking about you. He's proud of you and your boutique… Shoperapy, right?"

Ellie couldn't help but giggle at the mention of Chase.

"Oh, yeah, he just *loves* you!"

She exclaimed impulsively, the words bubbling forth before she could catch herself. Too much enthusiasm mixed with playful jest.

Ryan raised an eyebrow, slightly startled.

"Yeah... Chase is great."

"No, but Chase really loves you. Like, *really* loves you," Ellie insisted with misplaced enthusiasm.

The bemusement on Ryan's face was unmistakable as he chewed thoughtfully on his lip, trying to decipher her words. Too late she'd said far too much. The playful moment collapsed into awkward silence.

"Erm... so, the vandalism," the councillor interjected, seizing control.

Ellie tucked her hair behind her ear, mortified, silently wishing she'd paid more attention instead of oversharing Chase's affections.

As the meeting trudged along, Ellie found herself wishing she had paid more attention to the world around her instead of her phone, and maybe, just maybe, she should have been more discreet about Chase's affection.

As the meeting finally wrapped up, the warmth of her growing feelings for A.J. lingered.

Ellie gathered her things, laughter and embarrassment swirling together. She resolved to take charge of her life and her business—starting with focusing on the people right in front of her, before the sparkle of her distant mystery man stole her attention again.

But then the meeting took another turn.

Cameron fixed her with a teasing grin, arms crossed.

"And what do *you* think, Ellie?"

Her stomach dropped. She hadn't been listening at all. Caught red-handed, she forced what she hoped resembled an engaged smile.

"Yes, of course," she replied, the words landing with all the confidence of a bad punchline.

Cameron fixed her with a teasing grin, arms crossed. "And what do *you* think, Ellie?"

Her stomach dropped. She hadn't been listening at all. Caught red-handed, she forced what she hoped resembled an engaged smile.

"Yes, of course," she replied, the words landing with all the confidence of a bad punchline.

Cameron grinned wider. He knew.

"Great," he said, leaning back triumphantly.

"So, you'll take the first night watch?"

"Night watch.?"

Ellie's eyes widened as the realisation hit, her thoughts racing faster than ever. Me on night watch she thought as her heart beat faster.

CHAPTER 10: Lily

Lily was basking in the warm glow of Shoperapy. It truly was a hidden gem, tucked away from the bustling streets outside. The space buzzed with friendship and laughter as she settled in with Ellie and Grace for an exhilarating *girls' night in.*

They had assembled an eclectic collection of mismatched drinks: a fizzy elderflower cordial bubbling enthusiastically for Grace, a classic gin and tonic garnished with a slice of lime for Ellie, and Lily's adventurous tangerine mojito, sparkling under the shop's soft lights. Each sip felt like a small celebration, adding to the atmosphere swirling around them, perfectly complemented by the comforting scent of freshly baked pastries drifting through the air.

"What a perfect setup!" Ellie exclaimed, her voice rising with excitement as she spread her arms wide, gesturing s the charming table decorated with colourful fabric swatches and the prized silk-printing machine Teddy had generously lent them for the evening.

As ever, Teddy had been incredibly kind and supportive, which made Lily smile and frown at the same time. It was wonderful to have such a thoughtful *new* friend, yet the knowledge that she would soon be leaving tugged gently at her heartstrings.

"So, what's the first design?" Grace leaned closer, her eyes sparkling with curiosity and excitement, a playful grin tugging at her lips.

"Don't hold back! We want to see some real magic tonight. This is our creative night!"

Lily grinned, ready to impress the girls with her recent discoveries.

"Alright," she began, "I saw this unique pattern in a little shop on the boardwalk. It's inspired by the silk scarves that are popular in Dubai. They're stunning, aren't they?"

With a dramatic flourish, she spread the silks across the table. The vibrant fabrics shimmered under the bright lights like hidden treasures waiting to tell their stories. Each piece carried its own personality, infused with bold colours and playful patterns that perfectly reflected the spirit of the evening.

"Oh wow!" Grace exclaimed, reaching out to touch a vibrant blue piece adorned with swirling pink accents and hints of gold reminiscent of a desert sunset melting into twilight.

"This is gorgeous! I can't decide what we should create first. Should we go bold, or something more delicate and understated?"

Ellie's eyes practically danced with enthusiasm.

"You know, if these were available here, I bet women would absolutely adore them. They've never seen anything quite like this!"

She bounced slightly in her seat, already envisioning the endless possibilities and the appeal of Lily's designs.

"Right? And what's even better is that I can create my own custom patterns!" Lily replied, her voice bubbling with joy.

"We can all work on them together tonight. It'll be a celebration of friendship and creativity!"

A rosy glow crept across her cheeks, born from the excitement of crafting something unique alongside friends who believed in her and shared her infectious enthusiasm.

With a mischievous sparkle in her eye, Ellie raised her glass.

"To creativity and friendship! Here's to a night we won't forget!" Ellie declared.

The girls clinked their glasses together, the sound sparkling like their spirits as laughter erupted around the table.

"And to Teddy for this brilliant machine!" Grace added with a cheeky smile, her gaze drifting towards the intricate printing machine Teddy had generously gifted Lily.

"Let's not forget how lucky we are to actually be able to do this," Lily chuckled, though a quiet wave of melancholy washed over her. She knew, deep down, that the moment was fleeting.

Life had a funny way of reminding her that reality was waiting back in Dubai, its relentless demands already tugging at her, pulling her away from this carefree pocket of creativity.

The conversation flowed as effortlessly as the patterns spreading across the silks, punctuated by laughter and shared memories. Some moments bubbled with excitement as they debated which designs to print next, while others were peppered with hilarious anecdotes from their past mischief together. Lily felt a warmth bloom in her chest, wrapped in the comfort of friends who lifted her spirit and celebrated her ideas. As they rummaged through fabrics and sketches, each girl contributed her own inspiration, weaving their personalities into every piece.

Before long, they had produced several stunning printed scarves. The results were captivating, each one reflecting the essence of their friendship and shared creativity. As they admired their handiwork, pride swelled between them. The silks were vibrant, bold, and bursting with personality true expressions of the laughter, joy, and connection that had filled the room.

"See?" Ellie beamed, holding one of the prints up to the light.

"I told you they'd be a hit!"

She spun slightly, already caught up in the vision.

"We need to show these off. Let's do a little launch party an exclusive preview! I can just imagine the buzz!"

Her eyes gleamed with dreams of possibilities and excitement.

"Oh, what a beautiful dream," Lily replied softly. But beneath her smile, the thought collided with her growing reality, forming a cautious barrier between her hopes and the obligations waiting for her back home.

"Things just won't be like this when I go back, you know," she admitted quietly, the ache in her chest betraying her words. The bliss of the evening felt as though it were slipping through her fingers.

"But why not?" Grace shook her head in gentle defiance, tossing her soft curls with determination.

"Maybe we'll find a way somehow! It's all about making time and believing in ourselves!"

Her enthusiasm was infectious, tugging Lily back towards the warmth of the moment.

"Right," Ellie cut in with a grin, clapping her hands together. "Let's get these finished first… then we can think about world domination with silk scarves and a side of cheeky gossip."

Lily laughed, waving her hands playfully over the nearly completed prints, eager to chase away the creeping thoughts of reality and hold onto the magic of the night just a little longer.

As the evening wore on, the atmosphere shifted gently. Conversations ebbed and flowed between bursts of artistic focus and uncontrollable giggles. The demands of their everyday lives faded into the background as the prints came alive beneath their hands, while shared gossip drew them even closer. Lily cherished how effortless it felt to be surrounded by friends who celebrated every small spark of creativity and whimsy idea.

By the end of the night, a warm glow of satisfaction radiated through the circle of friends. All that remained was the grand unveiling of their finished scarves. Each scarf proudly displaying the unique touch and spirit each girl had woven into the stunning silk fabric.

A celebratory fashion show was the obvious next step. A chance to delight in their newfound skills and creativity.

But suddenly, a subtle change in the air drew Lily's attention.

"So," Grace said, winking as she leaned forward, her eyes sparkling with mischief and anticipation. "Who's next on the gossip train?"

She was always the one to lure the group into an exciting discussion or gossip, and Lily knew that look well.

"Speaking of gossip…" Lily began cautiously, steering the conversation back towards lighter, more tantalising territory.

"I ran into Sara the other day. And get this she was with a man. You will *not* believe it."

Ellie's interest heightened instantly, her eyes widening as she swivelled towards Lily.

"Spill! What do you mean, *with a man*? You cannot drop a bomb like that without explaining the details!"

"Oh, he was older, and might I add… rather attractive."

Lily replied, a mischievous glint dancing in her eyes as she replayed the moment in her mind,

Both girls leaned in.

"We're talking a proper silver fox… George Cloony springs to mind.

Well maybe not *that* old, but you know what I mean." Lily continued, warming to the role.

"Lovely hair, confident smile, and the kind of physique that suggested he spent more time at the gym than I do. You know… the *whole* package."

She could practically feel the excitement bubbling between them.

"What were they up to?" Ellie leaned in, her curiosity piqued to an uncontainable level as she took a sip of her drink, hanging onto every detail like it was a thrilling chapter in a novel.

Lily brought a finger to her lips, hesitating deliberately.

"You know… I probably shouldn't say," she teased, letting the suspense hang deliciously in the air.

Both girls narrowed their eyes at her in perfect synchrony, identical knowing smiles spreading across their faces.

"Oh no," Grace said firmly. "You cannot just drop that gem and stop there. Give us the tea."

With a cheeky laugh, Lily finally relented.

"Alright, alright. They were getting cosy on a bench at the park," she said, lowering her voice dramatically.

"Nestled close together…"

She paused for effect.

"Let's just say. they weren't *just* sharing a moment. There was… chemistry. The kind you can practically feel in the air."

Ellie clapped her hands together in delight.

"A scandal! This is juicy! Imagine if they were on a date oh, it's like something straight out of a film!"

Ellie's imagination ran wild as she conjured scenes of romantic rendezvous and secret meetings.

"Oh, totally!" Grace chimed in, practically bouncing in her seat.

"What if they're actually seeing each other? That would be something, wouldn't it? I'd love to see how that story unfolds!"

"Well, I can only imagine," Lily replied, her own excitement growing.

"She's been so secretive lately. It's either that… or he's a total nobody."

She shook her head with a grin.

"But trust me he did *not* look like a nobody. More like a mysterious bachelor, if you ask me. Teddy said his name was Charlie."

The girls exchanged delighted looks.

Sara had a man. But who was Charlie?

And when would they finally get to meet him?

Ellie, barely able to contain herself, immediately pulled out her phone and began texting Victoria.

> **E to V**: Wow, lucky you, Mamma.
> **V to E**: Hey, Ellie! What do you mean?
> **E to V:** A yummy boyfriend for Sara!
> **E to V:** How come you didn't tell?
> **V to E**: A yummy boyfriend for Sara?
> **E to V**: Oh, don't pretend like you didn't know
> **E to V:** I hear he's very handsome…

E to V: And older…
V to E: Is he now?
E to V: And even with a sexy name.
E to V: I think his name is Charlie.
V to E: Charlie! Are you serious?

CHAPTER 11: **Sara**

Sara and Victoria stepped into Shoperapy, the vibrant laughter from the café still lingering around them like a pleasant aura. They had just enjoyed a lovely lunch at their favourite spot, Ronzo, where Victoria had generously treated Sara to an indulgent spread of her favourite dishes: crispy vegetable tempura, a rich avocado salad, and a decadent chocolate torte that still left a hint of sweetness on Sara's lips. The afternoon had felt light-hearted and cheerful, yet beneath Sara's laughter, a small flutter of suspicion began to stir. Had her mother been unusually attentive today?

As they entered the shop, the familiar bell above the door chimed softly, announcing their arrival. Ellie looked up from behind the counter, her face instantly brightening.

"Back again, ladies? What brings you in this time?" she asked, a grin plastered across her face.

Sara chuckled lightly, brushing a stray strand of hair behind her ear.

"We seem to be here a lot lately, don't we?" she replied, her tone playful and casual.

Shoperapy had a magnetic pull, especially for mothers and daughters, but today something felt different. Beneath the usual comfort and familiarity, Sara sensed an undercurrent of hesitation. Why other than the simple allure of shopping were they here again so soon?

She glanced at Victoria and noticed the change immediately. Her mother's expression carried a nervous energy, the corners of her mouth twitching slightly, as if she were struggling to contain a secret.

It was then, with sudden clarity, that Sara realised something was amiss.

And just as the thought settled, Victoria dropped the bombshell.

Sara froze, her mouth falling open slightly.

"I do?" she blurted out, genuine shock coursing through her."

Stunned, Sara's mouth fell open slightly.

"I do??" she blurted out, genuine shock coursing through her.

The idea felt completely alien especially considering she was secretly seeing someone, a truth she had carefully tucked away and guarded with meticulous care.

"Yes!" Victoria chimed, her eyes sparkling.

"Just because you're pregnant doesn't mean you can't still find *the one*. There's simply more of you to love now!"

A heavy silence settled over the space, the words hanging awkwardly in the air. Sara shifted uncomfortably, her cheeks warming as she tried to process what she was hearing.

"Um… Mum," she said carefully, her voice faltering just slightly,

"I'm really not in a place where I want to date."

She needed to voice her discomfort, but her mother's relentless enthusiasm only seemed to steamroll over her reluctance.

"Nonsense!" Victoria dismissed, waving her hand as though brushing away Sara's concern like dust from a shelf.

"Once you try on the perfect date dress, you'll feel completely different. Trust me!"

Before Sara could protest further, she found herself reluctantly agreeing to try on a few outfits. Yet with every step she took towards the changing room, a seed of doubt took deeper root.

Was her mother's sudden enthusiasm simply a fixation on clothes and romance?

Or was there something else at play?

Why this abrupt interest in dating for a daughter who, not so long ago, had been focused solely on finishing her degree and preparing for motherhood?

As she sifted through racks of clothes, Victoria continued to push for something "younger," a fact that only deepened the furrow in Sara's brow.

"Sara, darling, you're so young. You don't want to look older than your years. There's plenty of time for that later. Enjoy your youth!"

Ellie, sensing the growing tension, decided to interject as she organised a new batch of chic scarves.

"So, Sara," she said lightly, "what do you know about this man you've been set up with?"

She was trying to keep the atmosphere relaxed, but the question stirred a gnawing unease within Sara. Had she even thought to ask about the date? The truth was, she couldn't bring herself to fully embrace the idea of dating right now especially when her heart already belonged to someone else.

Victoria quickly filled the silence, eagerness lacing her words.

"Oh, he's lovely! Really! Just your age, and at the same point in life as you are."

The way she spoke painted a picture of a perfect match, yet all Sara could focus on were the words *young* and *same age*. Suddenly, it felt as though Victoria was trying to steer her daughter towards a life she wasn't ready to step into.

"Just think about it," Victoria urged, turning to hold up a shimmering dress that had caught her eye.

"This would be perfect! Exactly the kind of dress a lovely young lady would wear on a romantic evening. You'll absolutely shine.""

With a reluctant sigh, Sara took the dress, the fabric soft beneath her fingers.

Maybe I should just tell her no, she thought.

She glanced back at her mother's beaming smile, the weight of expectation pressing down on her, weaving uncertainty, and curiosity together. She wasn't interested in a date she had Charlie. So, what exactly was her mum up to?

Sara stood in the dressing room, her heart racing as she fiddled with the hem of her top. Outside, Ellie chatted animatedly about the man Victoria had set her up with.

"Ellie," Sara whispered, leaning closer as the fabric curtain swayed slightly.

"Did Lily maybe tell you she saw me with someone… older at the beach?"

Ellie nodded, her expression shifting to one of concern. Sara swallowed and lowered her voice further.

"And did you maybe tell my mum…?"

"I'm so sorry, Sara," Ellie said quickly, her eyes widening in realisation.

"I didn't think it was a secret! I feel terrible."

Taking a slow breath, Sara felt a heavy knot settle in her stomach.

"I'm dating Charlie... my dad's best friend," she confessed quietly, glancing at her reflection in the mirror.

"He's much older, and I've been putting off telling my mum for ages. I just knew she wouldn't approve."

As Ellie processed this, Sara watched her expression shift from shock to empathy. The realisation hit harder than ever.

With this blind date business, it was painfully clear her mother did *not* approve of Charlie.

Great!

Blog
Posted: 4:43 AM (GMT)
User: Your Fashion Ellie-vator
Subscribers: 529

Heeeeeeelllllooooo YOU... yes, you, aaaaamazing people!

What a time we've had at Shoperapy! Not only have I put my big foot in it and caused a bit of upset (and yes, I'm feeling more than a little sick about it), but I've also somehow managed to get myself involved in catching a vandal.

It feels like an eternity since my days in Dubai with everything that's been happening here. And yes, I've agreed to host the very first community night watch alongside some fabulous friends! And because I don't do anything by halves, I've decided to add a touch of glamour to our watch. Everyone will be dressing up in our fabulous gowns to paint the town red, as they say!

I can hardly contain my excitement. Let's hope we shock the vandal before he gets the chance to paint the walls!

Have you visited Shoperapy recently? You must come and see our Autumn window display. Grace has been incredibly creative, and the clothes are simply stunning, perfect for anyone searching for that special outfit.

Pop in anytime to hear all the latest Meadowbank drama... and maybe leave with a gorgeous outfit for the perfect date.

See you all soon!
Much love
Ellie xx

CHAPTER 12: Ellie

Ellie stood behind the counter of Shoperapy, the soft hum of the ceiling fan unable to drown out the nagging feeling in her chest. She still felt awful about disclosing information to Victoria about Sara and Charlie. Her stomach twisted as she replayed the moment in her mind like a scratchy record.

What if she had caused a rift between friends? What was she supposed to do now? She thought.

The sparkle of the shop felt different today almost oppressive, like a heavy cloud hanging over her head.

Just as she was about to sink deeper into her thoughts, the bell above the shop door chimed with its familiar jingle. Ellie's heart skipped a beat as Amy stepped inside. The air felt charged, as if a portal had opened to a new dimension where hope lingered just out of reach.

Ellie's eyes widened in surprise. After the fiasco at the Autumn Open House, she had never expected to see Amy back amid all this sparkle ever again. Amy was notoriously cold and standoffish, dressed head-to-toe in a tailored black suit that seemed to wear her rather than the other way around. The contrast was almost comical as she stood there, looking thoroughly unimpressed by the surroundings bursting with colour.

"Can I help you with anything Amy?" Ellie asked, her voice rising above the hum of the shop as she tried to sound as enthusiastic as possible.

"No, I'm just looking," Amy replied curtly, her eyes narrowing as they darted around the shop, scanning for treasure among the racks of dresses and accessories.

"Really, I was just in the neighbourhood and thought I'd take a glance through. I'm not buying anything. Nope. Just a quick look."

The finality in her tone was unmistakable, yet Ellie couldn't shake the feeling that there was more to Amy's visit than mere curiosity.

Ellie nodded and returned to the counter, her mind still racing with guilt and anxiety. But it didn't take long for her to notice that Amy had lingered far longer than her words suggested. Something was amiss, and Ellie's curiosity began to itch. She had to find out.

A few moments later, her eyes landed on Amy, who wasn't really browsing the racks of beautiful clothes at all. Instead, she kept glancing towards the window, the one that had been vandalised the night before. Its shattered glass glinting ominously in the afternoon light.

At first, confusion washed over Ellie. Then, like a light bulb flicking on, realisation struck.

She's waiting for Noah the window cleaner.

Excitement bubbled up inside her, warming her chest. This was exactly what she wanted Shoperapy to represent: a place where women could find love whether love at first sight or love just for one unforgettable night. The thrill of potential matchmaking sent a shiver of delight through her.

What if this actually works? she thought, her heart racing.

She could hardly believe it. The seemingly closed book, Amy, appeared to be standing on the brink of romance. It almost felt too good to be true. The possibility of a blossoming connection set Ellie's imagination alight, determination surging through her veins.

Beaming, she grabbed her phone and began typing rapidly, firing off a message to Jess about the prospect. Together, they could help Amy connect with Noah. Even stiff, black-suited Amy could use a little help when it came to matters of the heart.

Just as Ellie hit send, she froze.

Her smile faltered as the realisation struck there was no getting that message back.

Had she shared another secret that wasn't hers to tell?

Anxiety clawed at her chest as she chewed on her lip, a painfully familiar sense of dread settling in. Once again, Ellie was left wondering whether she had just unleashed another wave of chaos—one she might not be able to stop.

Before she could settle her nerves, the door swung open again, this time with a more forceful clang. Chase stormed in, nearly ploughing straight into Amy, who quickly sidestepped with a startled look. He marched directly up to Ellie, his face a shade deeper than the crimson bags on display, his breathing erratic and uneven.

"Did you tell Ryan that I liked him?"

Chase nearly shouted, his voice tinged with urgency and a hint of panic.

Ellie's heart sank at the implication. She could already feel the weight of embarrassment creeping up her spine. Hesitating, her mind raced like a runaway train, grappling with the sudden tension in the air. Just as she was about to deny it, a flicker of realisation struck her like lightning. While distracted by her wild matchmaking ideas, she may have let something slip to Ryan about Chase. An involuntary wince crossed her face. She really had been putting her foot in it lately.

She could already see the scenario unfolding in her mind: Chase's feelings exposed, the delicate balance of their friendship wobbling because of her loose tongue.

"Maybe…" Ellie stumbled, glancing sideways as she searched for the right words, her throat tightening with each passing second.

"Did something bad happen?"

Chase's expression twisted into pure horror.

"Something horrible!" His eyes sparkled with distress as his hands clenched into fists at his sides.

Ellie felt the pit in her stomach deepen as she instinctively leaned in, desperate to calm him down.

"What do you mean?" she pressed, her own heart fluttering with apprehension, silently willing him to confide in her.

"The worst thing ever! Ryan asked me out!"

The words tumbled out in a cocktail of disbelief and alarm, as though Chase could no longer keep the secret bottled inside. The raw emotion in his voice struck Ellie so unexpectedly that laughter burst from her lips before she could stop herself, echoing around the shop.

"What's wrong with that?" she gasped, genuinely astonished. She hadn't expected this twist at all, and there was something almost absurdly funny about the way emotions tangled and collided in such a whirlwind.

As she looked at Chase more closely, a wave of understanding washed over her. He wasn't just upset; he was genuinely terrified. Ellie had never seen him like this before. It was as though he stood on the edge of an unfamiliar world, filled with vulnerability, and fear.

This wasn't a fleeting crush anymore. This was real. It was a leap into genuine feelings and possible commitment, and it left Chase exposed in a way he wasn't prepared for. Ellie could feel the weight of the moment pressing down on them both.

"I didn't mean for things to get so serious!" he blurted out.

"What if he doesn't like me back?"

The vulnerability in his voice cut deep. Ellie found herself wishing she could wrap him in reassurance, shielding him from every possible outcome.

"You'll never know unless you take the leap," she said gently, trying to steady him.

However, Chase was already spiralling, imagining a torrent of worst-case scenarios, awkward silences, and unrequited feelings, with each anxiety piling onto the one before it. His anxiety was palpable, sending Ellie's own thoughts racing.

Ellie was conflicted. Had she done the right thing by letting Ryan know about Chase's feelings? Was it truly her place to meddle in matters of the heart, or should she have stayed out of it entirely? How was she supposed to navigate these tangled webs of friendships and relationships without occasionally tripping over her own intentions?

Ellie sighed heavily, wishing for a wisdom that felt frustratingly out of reach, the burden of uncertainty weighing heavily on her shoulders.

Still, the thought of making things right filled her with renewed purpose.

With a plan slowly forming, Ellie glanced over towards Amy, who was still fixated on the vandalised window. There was an urgency about her stance, as though she were longing for something just beyond her reach, blissfully unaware of the emotional storm brewing.

Maybe she could help both friends.

Maybe just maybe, today could be a day of love at Shoperapy after all. A day of unexpected connections and repaired rifts.

In this whimsical world Ellie had created, anything felt possible if you dared to believe.

She set her thoughts into motion. She would bring everyone together and let them navigate this mess as a team. Love was complicated and messy but perhaps that was exactly how it was meant to be.

Later that evening, after closing the shop, Ellie settled onto her sofa. Her laptop warmed her knees as a familiar sense of comfort wrapped around her. She opened her email, spotting a new message waiting for her.

It was from the **Mystery Man from Dubai**.

From: A.J.
To: Ellie Edwards
Subject: Thinking of you
Ellie,
I've been thinking about your earlier musings on secrets. Have you been too loose with your lips? It's a tricky thing, isn't it? Sometimes, opening up too much can lead to unexpected outcomes.

Ellie chuckled softly, wonder flashing through her mind. Here was this enigmatic figure, showing such depth in his words.

From: Ellie Edwards
To: A.J.
Subject: Thinking of you
Maybe I have, but what about you? You must have a secret. Everyone does.

It intrigued her to think about the layers hidden behind his mysterious persona. Surely a man living in a place such as extravagant as Dubai had countless stories yet to be told.

A.J. replied almost immediately…

From: A.J.
To: Ellie Edwards
Subject: Thinking of you
I like your open and honest personality, Ellie. Secrets help no one. But I assure you, I want to have no secrets from you. You are energy incarnate, and I find it refreshing. It's better to not have secrets and take risks. Especially with love!
A.J.

This declaration pulled a smile from Ellie as she read those words, imagining the poetic tone in which they might have been delivered. It felt good to be appreciated for her true self, acknowledgement wrapping around her like a warm blanket on a wintry day.

From: Ellie Edwards
To: A.J.
Subject: Thinking of you
Then tell me your name.

From: A.J.
To: Ellie Edwards
Subject: Thinking of you

My name is Amir, but I will go by whatever name you wish to call me. The name you choose holds power, just as you do.
Amir

Ellie felt a warm flush rise in her cheeks. Who was this, Amir? What stories did he hold? Her heart fluttered at the idea of meeting this Mystery Man from Dubai… *Amir.*

CHAPTER 13: Amy

Amy sat at the polished wooden table in the bustling restaurant, her fingers drumming a silent tune against its surface as she observed the lively scene around her. The atmosphere was alive with laughter and the clinking of cutlery. Couples leaned towards one another in animated conversation, while families gathered as though celebrating something extravagant and joyous.

To Amy, a sit-down restaurant felt utterly absurd. Who wanted to sit around waiting for food to arrive? If she had her way, they would have grabbed a quick takeaway and spared her the boredom altogether. The entire scenario struck her as painfully tedious like watching paint dry in slow motion.

To distract herself from the clumsy small talk that would undoubtedly unfold once her friend arrived, Amy attempted to immerse herself in the extensive menu. The options blurred together as she scanned the list of dishes, desperately hoping something might spark even a flicker of interest. Her thoughts, however, drifted back to the reason she was here at all…to make an effort with Jess.

It hadn't helped that she'd left Shoperapy earlier than intended, cutting her visit short before Noah arrived to clean the window. Even now, the memory of her hasty departure lingered, vivid and uncomfortable.

She had lingered as long as she could, pretending to scrutinise sale items while her heart raced at the thought of Noah that idiosyncratic man with the easy smile and slightly tousled hair. The moment the door chimed to announce his arrival, her stomach had twisted with a familiar mix of excitement and embarrassment. Without thinking, she'd quickly fled, cursing her own silly hesitation.

Her pride simply wouldn't allow her to stay. Even though, deep in the hidden corners of her heart, she genuinely wanted to see him again. The thought alone felt ridiculous, let alone admitting it out loud.

Now, seated in the increasingly crowded restaurant, Amy glanced around at the sound of laughter and chatter, and couldn't shake the feeling of being out of place. It might have been heartwarming under different circumstances if not for her own simmering discontent and quiet envy of people who seemed so effortlessly connected.

She exhaled heavily and muttered under her breath.

Well, maybe I'm just one of those single women who can't handle it.

The voice echoed in her mind, an attempt to shake off the grumpiness that had settled stubbornly in her chest.

Just then, Jess breezed in, instantly drawing the attention of nearby diners with her warm, ringing laughter. Her hair flowed behind her, framing her cheerful face, and her bright, infectious smile seemed to light up the entire restaurant.

Spotting Amy, Jess waved enthusiastically before making her way over.

"Sorry I'm late! Traffic was madness," she declared, sliding into the chair opposite Amy with her usual confident ease.

"What did I miss?" she added, tilting her head with playful curiosity.

"You look like you're planning an escape."

The sparkle in Jess's voice only highlighted Amy's earlier irritation.

"Just the usual," Amy sighed, forcing a smile that felt tighter than she liked.

"I was just thinking about how much I dislike waiting for food."

The moment the words left her mouth, she regretted how sharp they sounded. Jess's raised eyebrow said it all.

Jess chuckled, her eyes twinkling with mischief, as though she'd just stumbled upon something mildly entertaining.

"Well, at least you've got me to keep you company," she said lightly.

"Let's order something tasty, shall we? I could eat a horse!"

The relentless enthusiasm in Jess's voice slowly began to soothe the growing impatience within Amy.

As they browsed the menu together, a gentle ease settled over her, the initial tension uncoiling like a tightly wound spring. Perhaps she had been too hasty in her judgement of this lunch meeting. Jess didn't push her to unpack personal woes, which Amy genuinely appreciated.

Despite her earlier doubts, laughter escaped her lips when Jess recounted a particularly embarrassing story involving a misplaced order at a corporate event a mix-up that had resulted in trays of delicious cupcakes being delivered to the wrong table and ultimately smashed during a minor office brawl.

Hours flitted by as they shared a platter of nachos piled high, glistening with melted cheese and spicy jalapeños, indulging in funny stories about Adam. The warm, indulgent bites offered unexpected comfort, allowing Amy to forget the agitation she'd felt only moments earlier. Jess's kindness and patience shone through every comment as she listened intently, and for the first time, Amy felt herself softening towards her friend.

Perhaps she could finally understand why Adam had taken such a liking to Jess.

The rigid assumptions Amy had clung to began to fade as she recognised the genuine bond forming between them. A shared history didn't have to breed animosity; it could nurture something far more grounding and sincere.

"You know," Amy began, her heart-warming slightly as she leaned closer towards Jess.

"When we were kids, Adam honestly believed he could take on a bear."

Jess raised her eyebrows in amused disbelief.

"He used to wear this ridiculous costume made from old pillows," Amy continued, a smile tugging at her lips, "complete with teddy-bear ears and everything. The whole neighbourhood thought he was a bit bonkers. Can you believe that?"

Jess laughed, the sound ringing out like music, an instant spark igniting between them.

"I can just picture it! And I bet he thought he was incredibly brave too…a little warrior battling imaginary creatures!"

"Exactly! Amy chuckled. "He'd dash around the garden, puffing out his chest like some cartoon superhero, shouting at anyone who dared challenge him. The kids from across the street would laugh, but he was relentless. Anyone who confronted 'The Bear' was warned just how tough he was."

She shook her head while laughing at the thought.

"Although, if I'm honest, it was mostly Adam tripping over himself. But he savoured every moment of it, fully believing he was indestructible."

Amy's laughter was contagious, spilling easily now.

As they finished the platter of nachos and prepared to move on to dessert, a gentle warmth enveloped Amy's heart a quiet appreciation blooming for this unexpected lunch and the connection she hadn't anticipated.

As if on cue, dessert arrived, rich chocolate mousse swirled like dark velvet, crowned with sprigs of fresh mint and a thick, creamy topping. The indulgence promised comfort, and for a moment, both women surrendered to it, digging in wholeheartedly, savouring every bite.

As Amy's gaze flicked towards Jess, she reflected on how this lunch had unexpectedly transformed into something genuine, a rare moment of connection that had gently pushed old grudges aside.

But just as the atmosphere seemed to sparkle with ease, everything shifted.

Jess leaned in a little closer, her expression bright and conspiratorial as she finished paying the bill.

"I heard from a little birdy that you've got a crush, Amy."

Amy's heart slammed against her ribs, heat rushing to her cheeks.

"What?"

The word came out sharper than intended. Her body tensed instinctively, stomach knotting as her mind raced.

Had someone said something? Did Ellie know?

"Oh, come on," Jess chuckled lightly, the teasing lilt scraping against Amy's already frayed nerves.

"Don't be embarrassed. I think Noah is totally cute!"

"Oh, for goodness' sake!" Amy blurted, disbelief flooding her voice.

"I have *no* interest in Noah. In fact, I actively dislike him. I'd be perfectly happy if I never saw him again."

The words spilled out messy and defensive, splattering the warmth of the moment with sharp-edged tension.

Jess's smile faltered, concern creasing her brow.

"I didn't mean to upset you," she said quickly, her voice softening.

"I was just joking. It was meant to be fun."

But it was already too late.

Amy's walls shot back up, thicker, and higher than before. She clammed up, trapped in the spiral of embarrassment and irritation. The warmth they'd built evaporated, leaving behind a heavy, awkward silence. What had felt like progress moments earlier now lay exposed and fragile, the unresolved feelings between them impossible to ignore.

Their goodbyes were stiff and uneasy, stripped of the laughter that had flowed so easily before.

"See you then," Amy muttered, stepping back from the table, desperate to escape.

Jess offered a faint smile that didn't quite reach her eyes, lifting a hesitant hand as Amy hurried out of the restaurant. The cool evening air hit her face, but it did nothing to ease the sense of defeat swelling in her chest.

As she wandered down the street, the lingering disappointment settled heavily on her shoulders, almost choking her. All the progress made towards understanding Jess seemed to dissolve into thin air. Their relationship, which had blossomed beautifully over lunch, now rested back at square one. All the progress she'd made towards understanding Jess felt undone, dissolved in a single careless moment. She exhaled slowly, wishing she could rewind time and swallow the words that had burst out in self-defence.

And yet, beneath the frustration, a faint undercurrent lingered. Something unfinished. Something unresolved.

Still, Amy squared her shoulders.

Whatever fragile bridge had formed between them was gone.

And she told herself… that was probably for the best.

Jess texted Ellie:

J to E: Well, I really messed things up at lunch with Amy. I brought up Noah, and I really shouldn't have. Things were going so well, but the second I mentioned him, everything turned sour again.

E to J: I'm sorry, Jess. I feel awful. I really need to learn when to keep my mouth shut.

Blog:
Posted: 9:06 PM (GMT)
User: Your Fashion Ellie-vator
Subscribers: 602

Draft 1: ~~Heeeeelloooo gorgeous people, so much has been happening… (no, I'm not sharing anything, about other people's lives.)~~ *Ellie thought to herself.*

Well, sorry, nothing much new to report.
Ellie xx

CHAPTER 14: Lily

The rain pelted against the windows of Lily's hotel suite, drumming a relentless rhythm that drowned out the excitement of the day they had planned. Lily stared out at the grey sky, her spirits sinking beneath the weight of the heavy clouds. She had been so looking forward to spending the day with her vibrant friend, Teddy. As droplets raced down the glass, it felt as though the world outside was mirroring her disappointment.

She turned to Teddy.

"Rain cannot stop us from having fun! Let's think of something else," Teddy said optimistically.

"What do you have in mind?" Lily asked, a spark of curiosity flickering despite her low mood.

She couldn't help smiling at the enthusiasm radiating from him. Teddy's optimism was unyielding, even when trouble loomed. Just seeing him there planted a small seed of hope in her chest, despite the gloom.

Teddy's eyes twinkled as he reached behind the cushions and pulled out a small, bright orange laptop, opening it with an exaggerated flourish.

"You should give me a tour of Dubai! You've been there for a while now, and I showed you my hometown before. It's only fair that you show me yours, don't you think?"

The idea glimmered like a ray of sunshine breaking through the clouds, igniting a flicker of excitement in Lily. She giggled, unable to suppress it. Teddy's enthusiasm was irresistible.

"That sounds fun, but there's just one little problem…" she said, gesturing dramatically towards the windows, where the downpour showed no signs of stopping.

"We're not in Dubai."

Teddy's grin only widened, his confidence completely intact.

"Not yet! We can do a virtual tour. Come on it'll be great!"

He shuffled closer, and his excitement proved contagious, softening her disappointment more than she expected.

With a soft sigh and a smile tugging at her lips Lily sank back onto the couch, resigned but intrigued. Teddy set the laptop on the coffee table beside a steaming mug of hot chocolate, its rich aroma wrapping around them like a warm hug. They ordered room service, piled pillows around themselves, and settled in for comfort.

Ed Sheeran played softly in the background, lulling them into a cosy bubble while the rain continued its steady rhythm outside. It felt as though they were cocooned in a world of their own, untouched by the rain.

"Alright then," Lily said brightly, clapping her hands once.

"Let's begin the tour."

She pulled up the presentation, eager to show off her temporary home. The opening image filled the screen. The hotel lobby, grand and gleaming with crystal chandeliers and plush sofas.

It was easy to describe.

"This is where I first arrived," she said animatedly. "It felt like stepping into a diamond."

Teddy listened intently, nodding along and soaking up every detail.

"And just over here," Lily added with a grin, "is where I discovered the *best* pastries."

She shifted the screen, revealing a mouth-watering display of fresh croissants and éclairs, their glossy layers almost leaping from the screen and tempting them both with thoughts of indulgence.

But as the tour continued, Lily's enthusiasm began to falter. She shifted nervously on the couch, suddenly aware of the need to keep things moving.

"And over there is the reception area where I check in," she said, her words beginning to rush. "It's really organised, and the staff are lovely."

The bubbling excitement from earlier had thinned, her voice no longer carrying the same sparkle.

As Teddy listened attentively, Lily felt her anxiety creep in. The sun-soaked beach day she'd imagined that morning felt impossibly distant now, as unreachable as the sunlight behind the storm clouds.

"Isn't it spectacular?" Teddy prompted, his tone warm and encouraging.

"Yes, well of course," Lily replied quickly, her mind racing ahead, searching for the next highlight she could offer.

"But I can't just keep talking about the hotel."

She drew in a steadying breath, summoning her courage.

"Next up is my apartment. It's just down the street from the hotel."

A photo of her flat filled the screen… small, simple, almost dwarfed by the grandeur of the hotel images before it.

"It's… nice," she said softly. "But not grand like this place."

Her voice dropped, self-consciousness bubbling to the surface.

"But I like it," she added quickly. "It's homely."

A flicker of longing stirred as she remembered how it felt to return there after long, exhausting shifts to the quiet, the familiarity, the sense of retreat.

"Homely is wonderful," Teddy said without hesitation.

"I love seeing where you live. I'd love to visit someday."

His sincerity was unwavering, yet Lily couldn't shake the gnawing feeling of inadequacy tightening in her chest. She paused, staring at the screen as a heavy expectation settled over her.

What else was there to show?

"But… what else?" Teddy asked gently, tilting his head, encouraging her to dig deeper.

Her heart began to race as she flicked through more images: the go-to restaurant where she grabbed quick meals between shifts; the small park just around the block where she occasionally stole a moment of quiet; the nearby coffee shop that served the best espresso.

Yet with every image, the same truth pressed harder against her chest.

Everything led back to the hotel.

The realization came slowly, uncomfortably, her life had narrowed, shrinking into a single orbit. Work. Rest. Repeat. Her world had been reduced to a handful of familiar streets and routines, all tethered to those same four walls.

As the screen shifted to scenes of Dubai's extravagant buildings, vibrant shops, fancy restaurants and endless stretches of colour, noise, and movement, the contrast stung. Teddy spoke with ease about his hometown, about places he knew, memories he carried, adventures he had lived.

And suddenly, envy bloomed where pride once lived.

She had poured herself into her work, convinced that fulfilment lived in responsibility, in effort, in endurance. And yet, faced with how little she truly knew of the city she called home; the truth settled heavily in her chest.

How could I live here and know so little? She had enjoyed her work, it had fulfilled her, but she had barely lived beyond it.

Her world, she realised, had grown far too small.

Lily spoke anxiously, her eyes scanning the screen as images of towering skyscrapers, a glamorous marina, and sunlit beaches flickered past a dazzling world she had lived besides, yet never truly entered.

The rest of the tour passed in a blur. Feelings of inadequacy rose quickly, pressing against her chest. Teddy noticed immediately, concern etching itself into his small features.

"Lily, it is okay if you do not know everything," he said gently.

"Everyone's journey is different."

His warmth softened her momentarily, but the ache lingered. Each vibrant clip revealed movement, colour, possibility, everything her own experiences felt stripped of by comparison.

When the tour finally ended, the silence felt heavier than the rain outside.

The music had faded into the background, and the steady drumming on the windows echoed her unease, syncing with the quickening beat of her heart. The day she had imagined light, comforting, easy had transformed into something else entirely. Reflection. Restlessness.

Overwhelmed, Lily stood suddenly.

"I'm so sorry, Teddy, but I need to cut this short," she blurted, her voice sounding distant even to herself.

"But we can keep going," Teddy protested, worry shining in his button eyes. His heart always seemed bigger than his body.

"No, it's fine. Really. You should head back," she said quickly.

"I've got some laundry to take care of."

The excuse sounded hollow, even to her ears. She forced a smile, but it wavered, fragile under the weight of everything she wasn't saying.

Teddy studied her, torn between respecting her space and protecting her feelings.

"I think we should talk about whatever is bothering you," he said softly. "I don't want to go."

She shook her head, feeling heat rise to her cheeks with the urge to be alone.

"No. Really. You must go," she insisted, urgency creeping into her voice.

"I just need some time by myself, okay?"

The words spilled out harsher than she intended.

She ushered him towards the door, her chest tightening as his shoulders slumped.

"But... I'm still here for you," he said quietly, sadness threading through his voice.

"Just go, Teddy."

The moment the words left her mouth, regret followed. This was the last thing she wanted, to push away someone who cared. The rain continued its steady rhythm, her heart echoing every beat.

Teddy lingered once more before sighing, resigned. He looked back one last time.

"I'll be waiting for our next adventure," he said, hope clinging to his words as the door clicked shut behind him.

The sound landed heavier than she expected.

Alone, Lily sank back onto the sofa. The rain no longer soothed her; it pressed in, amplifying the thoughts she had long ignored.

For the first time, she did not find comfort in the sound of the rain; instead, a stirring within her grew… What if it was time to seize life beyond her work? What if there were adventures waiting to unfold? The potential of exploring both her local surroundings and the possibilities of undiscovered adventures floated through her mind, calling for her to break free from the confines of her routine.

As the rain continued its melancholic dance outside, a flicker of determination ignited within her. She resolved to find a balance, to not merely live inside the confines of her job. It was time to embrace the adventures in both Dubai and her own life, where every corner held a story yet to be told. Perhaps a new journey was waiting to unfold beyond the hotel walls, calling her to step outside, rain or shine inviting her to plunge into the richness of life's experience that hummed, waiting to be embraced.

Without giving herself time to second-guess it, Lily booked a ticket to Dubai.

Dear customer,

Thanks for your booking – your flight is confirmed, and your itinerary is below.

Edinburgh to Dubai 7:30pm arriving 12:45am

We are looking forward to welcoming you on board.

The Emirates team

CHAPTER 15: **Sara**

While Sara felt truly glamorous in the stunning, flowing navy dress that her mum and Ellie had helped her choose for her blind date, a flicker of regret tugged at her heart. She could not shake the persistent thought that it was Charlie she wanted to impress, not some stranger whose name she had only learned that morning. The dress hugged her curves, the flowing skirt billowing slightly as she moved, making her feel as though she were stepping out of a fairy tale. Yet as she stood before the restaurant, a quaint little bistro adorned with glowing fairy lights and bustling with life she bit her lip, wondering if perhaps she should have chosen honesty with her mum from the start. Why had she agreed to this scheme, this blind date that felt more like a trap than an opportunity for romance?

Sara had spent countless hours fantasising about a future with Charlie, her heart yearning for a love that felt vivid and real. Thoughts of their tender moments together made her stomach flutter with excitement and anxiety in equal measure. And yet, here she was, about to meet Mark, a man she had never laid eyes on before. The thought made her stomach churn, filling her with dread. She felt guilty yet conflicted. Should she confess her feelings for Charlie to her parents now, or would that only complicate things further? What if they didn't approve? What if they thought she was reckless, too young to truly understand love?

Taking a deep breath, she pushed open the door and stepped into the inviting warmth of the restaurant. The aroma of garlic bread and fresh herbs wafted through the air, momentarily distracting her from the anxious flutter in her chest. As she scanned the room, the soft glow of chandeliers cast an intimate light over the diners. Amid the cheerful clinking of glasses and bursts of laughter, she finally spotted Mark, seated at a table, a nervous smile playing on his lips.

He stood as she approached, instinctively revealing his gentlemanly nature as his eyes lit up in recognition. He leaned in to kiss her cheek softly, a gesture that managed to be both sweet and slightly awkward, before pulling out her chair with a flourish that made her feel oddly comforted, yet unsettled.

"Hi, I'm Mark," he said, his voice warm and inviting, though tinged with a hint of apprehension.

"Hi, I'm Sara," she replied, forcing a smile even as her heart raced. Her cheeks warmed beneath his gaze, and she fiddled with the delicate chain around her neck, a nervous habit that surfaced whenever she felt tense.

His eyes drifted to her dress, taking in every detail with clear appreciation.

"Wow, you look lovely. That colour suits you perfectly," he complimented.

"Thank you," she murmured, her blush deepening.

She wanted to believe it was the dress that made her feel beautiful, but deep down she knew it was the anticipation of spending time with Charlie that had once given her a spark — a spark she did not feel now.

They exchanged pleasantries, and as Mark commented on the crisp autumn evening.

"Isn't it simply perfect? The cool air makes it feel magical!"

A suffocating sense of urgency tightened around Sara's heart, squeezing with each passing moment.

She had to say something. She needed to let him know where she stood before this date spun completely out of control.

"Actually, before we get too comfortable…" Sara hesitated, glancing down at her plate as though it might hold the answer.

Before she could fully process it, the words tumbled out, spilling from her lips before she had the chance to stop them.

"I'm seeing someone."

Mark blinked in surprise, his brow furrowing as confusion washed over his features.

"Um… sorry, what?"

Sara felt an unsettling mix of panic and relief as she realised, she could not keep her secret locked away any longer. Seeing the genuine bewilderment in Mark's eyes made her heart ache, remorse settling in as she recognised the awkward position, she had placed him in. He seemed like such a decent guy, and the last thing she wanted was to hurt him. Taking a deep breath, she steadied herself against the tide of emotions threatening to spill over.

"Look, I'm sorry. It's just… I feel like I need to be honest with you," she said softly, her voice barely rising above the gentle music drifting through the restaurant.

"Do you see those two people?"

Mark nodded slowly, still trying to process her earlier confession.

"That's my mum and my dad," she continued, her voice wavering slightly.

"They barely speak but they both don't approve of my relationship with Charlie. They think he's too old for me. He's a friend of theirs, and this" she gestured faintly between them, "is their way of trying to change my mind."

As she spoke, a warmth spread through her chest relief born from finally telling the truth.

"It's just that I really do like him," she went on, her voice trembling ever so slightly.

"I thought that if I went along with this blind date, it might convince them that I didn't know what I was doing. Maybe they'd see that I was too young to understand love." She inhaled sharply. "But the truth is, I think I might really be falling for him."

Mark absorbed her words, his expression softening as he listened. Who could fault someone for wanting their feelings to be respected? He leaned back in his chair, allowing the weight of the moment to settle.

"To be honest," he finally said, "I only did this as a favour to my aunt."

"Aunt?" Sara echoed, surprised.

"Yeah," he explained, lowering his voice conspiratorially. "She knows Victoria from the gym and thought I needed a push back into dating. I barely have time as it is I'm trying to get my business off the ground."

"Wow, what kind of business?" Sara asked, genuinely intrigued and quietly grateful for the shift away from her confession.

Mark leaned forward, his entire demeanour transforming as he began to speak passionately about his project.

"I'm starting a small tech company, focusing on apps that help improve mental wellbeing," he explained, his eyes brightening with enthusiasm.

"You wouldn't believe how much potential there is in helping people manage stress and anxiety. It's something I'm truly passionate about."

As Mark delved into the details of his venture, Sara could hardly believe how easy it had become to talk to him. It was refreshing to hear someone share their goals in such a compelling and genuine manner.

The evening continued to unfold pleasantly. Dinner arrived, and they bonded over their shared experiences. Sara finally allowed herself to gush about Charlie, her feelings spilling forth after months of keeping them bottled up, fearing her parents' disapproval. Mark listened intently, his eyes widening as she described her dreams for the future and the tender moments they had shared together.

"Honestly, it's refreshing to hear," he said, a genuine smile lighting his face. "You two sound wonderful together, and it's clear how deeply you care for him."

"Thanks," Sara replied, warmth blossoming in her chest. "I sometimes wonder if it's too soon to think about the future, but… everything feels so right between us."

She felt emboldened by the openness of the conversation, encouraged by how Mark simply welcomed her truth without judgment.

"Charlie is sweet, funny, and incredibly supportive. He is there for me in ways I never expected. It's like he truly sees me. Oh… and he's extremely attractive too." Sara said with a gleam in her eye.

With a newfound lightness in the atmosphere, Sara felt comfort blooming inside her.

"What about you and your aunt, then?" she asked, glad to shift the focus back to him and step away from the confessions that had taken so much courage to share.

He chuckled appreciatively.

"Honestly, my aunt just likes playing matchmaker. But she means well. She's a force of nature, always pushing me to get out there, which I appreciate, even if it's a bit overwhelming."

"I can understand that" Sara smiled. "Family can be intense sometimes."

The two of them continued chatting, their mutual understanding wrapping around them like a warm blanket, carrying them away from the anxieties that had shadowed the evening. They shared stories about childhood, aspirations, and even hidden talents, until the restaurant began closing for the night. What had initially felt like a forced encounter had blossomed into something unexpectedly enjoyable.

As they stepped out into the crisp night air, a gentle breeze playing with her hair, Mark turned to Sara with a grin.

"I'm really glad we met tonight," he said, his voice warm and sincere, making her feel as though they had forged a genuine bond, even in the unusual circumstances of their meeting.

"Me too," Sara replied, her heart feeling unexpectedly light as they walked down the street together. She felt grateful for the evening and the unexpected friendship that had emerged, knowing that she could return to Charlie with clarity and confidence, ready to share her heart fully without the weight of judgment pressing down.

In a world where secrets can become burdens too heavy to carry, embracing her truth had given her the clarity she so desperately sought. Looking back at her parents across the restaurant, smiling, and animatedly discussing something, she realised that their bond might finally be mending. That small miracle filled her with hope, encouraging her to believe that love could heal broken hearts and foster a brighter future.

As they reached a fork in the road, Sara paused, turning to Mark, her voice sincere.

"No, thank you. You reminded me of the value of connection, even during blind dates," Mark smiled.

"Maybe we could catch up again, as friends?" he suggested, sparking a thrill within her. Sara nodded enthusiastically.

"Absolutely!" she affirmed.

As she waved goodbye to Mark that evening, she realised that some connections, however unexpected, could offer invaluable lessons in honesty, friendship, and courage in the face of vulnerability. What had begun as an obligatory blind date transformed into the beginning of a new understanding not just of herself, but of the bonds formed while navigating the twists and turns of adolescence and love.

Later that night, when Sara's mum called to ask how the date went, Sara could honestly reply that it had been genuinely nice… and that she had made a new friend.

"Not boyfriend then?"

"Sorry, mum."

Victoria sighed to herself. The game continues.

From: Ellie Edwards
To: AJ
Subject: Just a Thought!
Hi Amir,
I hope you've had wonderful day in hot Dubai. I love hearing from you. This morning, I caught myself smiling at your casual promise that 'love always finds a way.' I must secretly believe in love since I can't resist emailing you.

From: A.J.
To: Ellie Edwards
Subject: Ref.: Just a Thought!
Evening Ellie,
Aren't you the one who's sworn off Cupid?

From: Ellie Edwards
To: AJ
Subject: Ref.: Just a Thought!
Ha ha, perhaps you've changed my mind, Amir. Maybe I could make an exception for you.

From: A.J.
To: Ellie Edwards
Subject: Ref: Just a Thought!
Then we will find a way, Ellie! Let's plan all our adventures, starting with you visiting Dubai again. It'll be your first taste of my world.

Ellie's heart raced at his suggestion. Could this really be happening?

From: Ellie Edwards
To: AJ
Subject: Ref: Just a Thought!
I will think about it. Or maybe you could come to Scotland???
Sorry I must go. Fashion is calling!
Chat soon.
Ellie

CHAPTER 16: Ellie

Ellie dimmed the lights at Shoperapy, her shadow dancing around the aisles of stylish clothes like a mischievous spectre. She wore a stunning gold sequin evening gown that shimmered softly in the darkness, catching glints of light from her trusty flashlight.

The elegance of the shop, laden with evening gowns and chic accessories, set the perfect backdrop for the evening's quirky theme. Ellie took a deep breath, letting herself soak in the joy of throwing such a unique event.

Tonight was an incredibly special kind of party, one that required absolute silence and stillness. This was no ordinary soiree; it was a stakeout party, intended to catch the vandal who had been turning the local businesses into makeshift canvases for graffiti. The community had been in an uproar, with every business owner sharing their exasperation and fears about the sudden onslaught of spray paint. Ellie decided something truly radical had to be done.

The evening gowns everyone would be wearing were accessorised with cute black hats and silk scarves emblazoned with words like "Justice," "Community," and "Stakeout Crew." These playful touches highlighted camaraderie among her friends while adding a fair dash of flair to their undercover mission.

"Oh, just imagine the scandal," she chuckled to herself, her mind alight with visions of neighbourhood gossip centred around their unconventional gathering.

"Being caught in a dress at a stakeout! Perhaps it will even become a new trend… Operation Glamorous Spy!"

There was something delightfully absurd in the notion of elegance meeting espionage. Glancing around the shop, she mentally approved of how it had transformed into a posh hideout, complete with all the drama one might find in a heist film.

To keep the mood playful, she had even ordered opera glasses instead of binoculars for her guests. 'Because who wouldn't want to snoop in style?' she mused, adjusting her sleeves with a flourish as she imagined the fun they would have while keeping a watchful eye on the street. She could already picture herself peering through the shimmering lenses, ready to catch the culprit in the act, all while looking undeniably fabulous.

However, as the clock ticked away and minutes stretched into what felt like hours, Ellie's excitement wavered, an unwelcome knot forming in her stomach. She peered through the shop window, her pulse quickening with each passing moment. What if she was the only one at this quirky party? What if everyone decided not to come because she had inadvertently spilled their secrets? Could she really blame them? Perhaps she had crossed a line.

Supporting one another, being there for each other, and creating a safe space for honesty were principles she had always cherished. Yet tonight, those beliefs felt more like hefty weights chained to her ankles. Doubt gnawed at her heart as she cast one last hopeful glance at the door.

Just as the second hand ticked into the quarter hour, the shop door swung open with a soft chime, jolting her from her thoughts. One by one, her friends began to arrive: Grace, with a sly grin that hinted at her excitement; Chase, looking slightly bemused as he adjusted his black hat; and the ever-dramatic Victoria, sporting an oversized hat that seemed to take on a life of its own as it bobbed with her every move. Sara stumbled in behind them, giggling, along with Jess and Amy, who glowed with happiness at the whimsical premise of the event.

"I do love a party where I don't have to talk," Amy declared, her eyes sparkling with mischief, a gleam that echoed through the quiet room. The nervous tension that had hung over Ellie dissipated, replaced by the light-hearted atmosphere enveloping the shop.

As the ensemble gathered, the room filled with soft giggles and playful banter, enhancing the jovial mood.

"Whose idea was it to wear these fabulous dresses when we're supposed to be spies?" Grace quipped, twirling in her gown as the sequins caught the light. The laughter that followed warmed Ellie's heart, banishing the self-doubt she had felt just moments ago.

Ellie felt a wave of relief. As the group embraced the absurdity of their circumstances, she noticed her friends genuinely enjoying themselves.

"I have to admit," Ellie said softly, "this is more fun than I could have ever imagined."

The realization struck her: the party had evolved into something richer than a mere mission. They were rediscovering the joy of friendship amidst the chaos surrounding them.

Encouraged, Ellie helped her friends adjust their 'stakeout uniforms,' arranging scarves and hats just so. They settled along the big windows, their sleek black silhouettes blending into the dim shop ambiance as they focused intently on the darkened street outside. A comfortable rhythm emerged, each glance a silent communication filled with unspoken camaraderie.

Occasionally, Ellie would catch a playful wink from Victoria or a teasing shake of Grace's head, and a wave of warmth wrapped around her heart. They had taken the unconventional nature of the evening and turned it into a bonding experience, etched in their laughter and mutual support.

Then the moment came. The unmistakable sound of scuttling noise outside, a shadow darting past a nearby shop. Time stood still as their hearts raced in unison. Ellie held her breath, opera glasses poised and ready, excitement bubbling just under the surface.

"Is that...?" Chase whispered, his eyes wide with anticipation.

But before they could react, the shadow disappeared, leaving only the lingering thrill of the chase. Ellie sighed, a mixture of frustration and exhilaration washing over her. Yet as she glanced at her friends, their eyes sparkling with delight, she realized they had not only orchestrated a brilliant plan to catch a vandal but had rekindled something far more meaningful: their shared spirit of adventure and mutual support.

And so, they waited silent, still, ready to catch a vandal while weaving closer connections among one another. Ellie realized that the essence of community truly lay in these moments of shared experience.

Then she noticed something: Lily was missing. Furrowing her brow, Ellie fished out her phone, fingers trembling slightly as she dialled her friend's number, hoping for a familiar voice.

To her astonishment, when the line connected, a cheerful voice chirped back,

"Hello!"

But the tone was not what Ellie expected; it was overly bright, almost unnaturally carefree.

"Are you at the airport?" she blurted, disbelief and annoyance bubbling just beneath her calm exterior. How could Lily just leave without a word?

"Yep! I'm off!" Lily replied, her enthusiasm palpable, as carefree as a bird in flight.

"Leaving a whole week before my scheduled departure! Change of plans, you know?"

There was a slight exuberance in her voice, but it only deepened Ellie's unease. This wasn't like Lily at all. Why hadn't she said anything beforehand? Had Ellie's recent stress about her own life somehow pushed Lily to make such a drastic decision?

Ellie's heart sank at the thought.

"Is this because of me?" she asked, biting her lip nervously, her stomach knotting. She couldn't shake the feeling that her own worries might have driven Lily to act suddenly.

"Definitely not! I just need to find home, Ellie. Find what it truly means to me."

There was a hint of whimsy in Lily's voice, as if she had just discovered a hidden joy in the world. Ellie felt a mix of happiness for Lily's newfound confidence and frustration at being left in the dark.

Now Ellie faced a dilemma. She needed to call Teddy to warn him about Lily's sudden departure. Yet as she paced her boutique, a nagging thought crossed her mind: she had promised not to meddle in her friends' affairs or share their secrets. This was becoming a tangled web of loyalty and instinct to protect.

"But this one could be vitally important!" Ellie scolded herself inwardly, fingers brushing through her hair as she weighed her options. With a resigned sigh, she drew in a deep breath, the weight of the decision pressing down on her shoulders.

"Okay, Ellie, this is the last, last time," she muttered, hoping it wouldn't become a recurring theme in her life.

Finally, she dialled Teddy's number, a mix of dread and determination settling in her chest. After all, friends looked out for each other even if it meant stepping into murky waters.

"Teddy, you need to know" Ellie began, bracing herself to deliver the news.

"It's Lily. She's going back to Dubai… she's at the airport…"

Ellie felt her phone go quiet…

CHAPTER 17: Lily

Lily sat in the crowded terminal, glancing at her watch for what felt like the hundredth time. Her heart raced as she realised that boarding for her flight to Dubai was starting soon. She was both excited and anxious; while she longed to return to her job, the flashy cityscape felt stark against the warmth of the connections she'd made in these small-town connections she was beginning to treasure more than her work. The thought of leaving Ellie and Teddy filled her with a gnawing anxiety she couldn't shake.

If only she'd taken more time to explore her own hometown instead of diving straight into work after returning to Dubai after University, then perhaps she wouldn't feel so restless, so out of place in the environment she had grown up in. Her job, with all its glitz and glamour, had always seemed like it would fulfil all her dreams, yet lately it felt more like an anchor dragging her down, a heavy weight on her shoulders.

"It's demanding… but do I even love it anymore?" she wondered, biting her lip and fidgeting restlessly in her seat. Too many late nights spent wrapped up in work instead of embracing life had left her stomach knotted with unease. She had made choices she intended to rectify but how could she, feeling so conflicted?

Just as she resolved to gather her thoughts and stand in line to board, she caught sight of a familiar face darting through the bustling crowd. Teddy, red-faced and breathless, was making his way towards her, weaving through the throng like a determined little ship navigating rough seas.

"Teddy! What are you doing here? How did you even know I was here?" she exclaimed, refusing to soften her stance. Surely, he must have been tipped off by Ellie, her playful yet persistent little friend! But that only added to her frustration.

"It doesn't really matter how," Teddy panted, a grin plastered across his face as he caught his breath. Lily wasn't convinced. She crossed her arms defiantly, narrowing her eyes at him in mock accusation.

"Ellie told you, didn't she?"

"Erm… maybe," he admitted, sheepishly running a hand through his ruffled hair. "But that's not important! I bought a ticket to Dublin just to get past security and talk you out of leaving."

"Wow, how romantic!" she teased, the corners of her mouth twitching despite her initial irritation. She felt a little lighter at his concern, yet her resolve remained firm. He had come to stop her, and while it was sweet, she was ready to leave.

"Teddy, listen," she began, her voice dropping an octave as the gravity of her decision settled around them like a heavy blanket.

"I've realised that I don't even know my hometown the way I should. This place," she gestured widely to the terminal, filled with travellers, families, and excitement, "it's just a backdrop to a life I haven't actually lived. I can't go back to being just a hotel guest in my own town, floating through it anonymously."

He fell silent for a moment, his brow furrowing as he processed her words.

"I get it, but I thought you weren't supposed to leave till later," he said, his gaze searching hers for some glimmer of hope, the desperation beginning to seep through his bravado.

"That was before I knew all the work I needed to get done!" Lily replied, her cheeks flushing. The weight of her responsibilities pressed heavily against her chest, as if the very air around her had thickened with duty.

Teddy frowned, deep in thought, his expression flickering with determination.

"But I haven't shown you everything yet!" He stepped closer to her, eyes sparkling as if they contained secrets waiting to be unveiled, the glimmer of adventure beckoning them both.

"The airplane is calling for the last group to board," she said reluctantly, her resolve starting to waver as the announcement echoed over the speakers, mingling with the sounds of rolling luggage and hurrying passengers.

"You've shown me a million things, and I'm so grateful, but surely there can't be anything at all left that we missed while I've been here."

Warmth bloomed in her chest as she thought of their shared adventures and late-night chats the laughter over mugs of steaming coffee, the moments of quiet understanding.

As she leaned in to kiss Teddy's cheek goodbye, a sudden thought struck him.

"What about the Castle?" he blurted out, his eyes wide and sincere.

"You can't leave without visiting…" desperation threading through his voice.

Lily paused, turning her head to look over her shoulder at him, the provocative suggestion hanging in the air like a tantalising invitation.

"The Castle?"

"Yes! The Castle! You don't want to leave without seeing it!"

His enthusiasm was contagious, and though Lily knew in the back of her mind that the Castle was merely a distraction from their conversation, she couldn't help but feel a flutter of excitement at the thought. How much he cared for her stirred something deep within a warmth that brought a reluctant smile to her lips.

"Oh, fine!" she sighed, relinquishing some of her bravado.

"Is it really that nice?"

The way Teddy beamed lit a spark of hope within her, illuminating the dreary reality she had been contemplating.

"The nicest castle in the world! You'd be kicking yourself for the rest of your life if you left before seeing it."

His eyes sparkled with a mixture of determination and charm, urging her to stay just a little longer.

A smile broke across Lily's face as something shifted within her when she met Teddy's gaze—it was nothing short of magnetic.

"Alright then," she said, her heart softening as the thought of spending a little more time with Teddy felt, oddly, necessary.

"I'll see the Castle, and then I'll go back."

The promise sounded tentative yet hopeful, as though she was willing to risk just a few more hours in this new chapter of her life.

Relief flooded Teddy's expression, and he took her bag from her, gesture after gesture turning into a gentle insistence that spoke of their blossoming connection. They began to walk together, the kinetic energy between them palpable as the boarding doors started to close.

"Castle and then back, that's a deal!" he said, taking her hand in his.

As they moved away, briskly heading towards the adventure that awaited them, Lily felt a sense of contentment she hadn't realised she had been missing. The hum of the airport faded into the background, overshadowed by the warmth of Teddy's hand in hers. She wasn't just a visitor anymore; she was part of something—a community that tugged at her heartstrings more than any job ever could.

Lily was going to strangle Ellie... but maybe she had done the right thing. Time would tell.

CHAPTER 18: Sara

Sara was in the midst of her afternoon routine, sprawled across her couch with a cup of tea in hand, when her phone buzzed insistently against the table. The screen lit up with her mum's name, and she rolled her eyes, wondering what could possibly be urgent enough for a call at this hour.

"Hello?" she answered, trying to mask the irritation in her voice. Her mind flickered to the list of chores she had hoped to tick off today: laundry, a bit of shopping, maybe even a walk.

"Sara, darling! You need to come to Shoperapy, it's a fashion emergency!"

Victoria's voice was frantic, laced with a hint of barely concealed laughter, creating a wave of worry in the pit of Sara's stomach.

"What's happened now?" Sara replied, curiosity piqued despite her initial annoyance. Shopping emergencies were hardly career-defining events.

"It's me! I tried on this dress, and I cannot get it off! I'm stuck, and I'm too embarrassed to call for help," Victoria managed to say between giggles.

In that moment, Sara could not help but imagine her mother floundering in the boutique, a victim of poorly fitting fashion.

Sara laughed, picturing her mum engulfed in a too-small dress, flailing about in some kind of polyester prison.

"Alright, I'm on my way!" she said, shaking her head in affectionate disbelief at her mother's antics.

After a short drive, her thoughts buzzing with what she might find, she dashed into the boutique. Her heart raced from both excitement and a tinge of worry. However, what she saw stopped her in her tracks. The boutique had been transformed into a kaleidoscope of joy! Balloons floated lazily overhead, twinkling streamers shimmered in the soft light, and stuffed animals adorned every available surface. It was as if she had stepped straight into a dream, drenched in pastel hues and cheerful decorations.

Victoria, Grace, Ellie, Lily, Jess, and surprisingly even Amy were gathered together, their faces alight with wide smiles, practically vibrating with anticipation.

"Surprise!" they chorused, their joy radiating through the boutique, and Sara's heart swelled as the warmth of their affection enveloped her something she had not expected on what she had assumed would be a rather dull afternoon.

"Whoa! A baby shower?" Sara exclaimed, her surprise quickly overshadowing her concern for her mum. She glanced around, taking in the delightful chaos of wrapped gifts and bright decorations, her mind racing to piece together who had orchestrated such a charming event.

"Yep! We planned it all while you were oblivious at home. Now that you're about to embark on this amazing journey, we couldn't wait any longer!" Ellie grinned, holding out a platter of delectable finger sandwiches and cupcakes.

As she settled onto one of the luxurious velvet couches, Sara felt the warmth of this community surround her. Laughter erupted as they engaged in baby shower games, including hilarious guessing games and silly charades each one more entertaining than the last. It felt surreal, an afternoon filled with teasing remarks, happy chatter, and the overwhelming compassion of her friends. Each moment felt like a precious treasure, the kind that seeped into her heart and made it blossom.

"Alright, ladies! Time to open gifts!" Grace declared, clapping her hands together with excitement, while Jess took charge of snapping photos to capture the ecstatic expressions.

One by one, the girls handed her beautifully wrapped presents, each more delightful than the last. There was a hand-knitted blanket adorned with tiny elephants, crafted by Ellie's mum; a lovely memory book decorated with stickers and glitter from Lily; and even an amusing collection of baby-themed novels from Jess, filled with stories of adventurous parenting. Sara couldn't remember feeling this happy surrounded by such am amazing group of women.

However, amid the bubbling laughter and sweet treats, Victoria's comments filtered through her mind like pesky clouds drifting across a bright sky. The banter surrounding the gifts became a curious background hum as Sara felt the air grow thick with unspoken tension.

"Honestly, at your age, I can't imagine caring for a child," Victoria mused, a smirk creeping across her face as she handed Sara an exceptionally posh stroller.

"But see, darling? You'll never need a rich, old man to take care of you because you have me!"

A pang shot through Sara. She knew the *rich, old man* Victoria was alluding to was Charlie the very thought sending a bittersweet shiver through her heart. It hurt more than she cared to admit, a knot of confusion and sadness tightening her chest.

"Thanks, Mum. It's lovely!" she replied, forcing a smile and a shrug, desperately trying to appear grateful.

"Of course, darling! You'll be the best mum!" Victoria continued, oblivious to the tightness growing in Sara's throat, her enthusiasm unwavering. As she looked around at her friends, buzzing with excitement, Sara found it difficult to reconcile the joy of the day with her turbulent feelings.

Inside, Sara wrestled with a whirlwind of emotions. One moment she was excited about the love surrounding her, and the next, her heart ached for Charlie. He had whispered the words "I love you" just last night. It had been perfect and tender, a moment she wanted to hold in her heart forever.

But her parents didn't understand. No matter how much Sara longed for their approval, she knew they wouldn't accept Charlie. Their dismissive remarks replayed in her mind, casting shadows over the brightness of the afternoon. Why couldn't they see how real their love was? It felt suffocating and isolating, the weight of unspoken expectations shaping every interaction.

"Hey, are you alright?" Jess asked, squeezing Sara's shoulder gently, breaking her reverie. The genuine concern on her friend's face pulled Sara back to the moment, allowing her to relax slightly.

"Yeah! Just… thinking about stuff," Sara replied, forcing a smile that felt feeble at best while desperately trying to appear nonchalant.

As the afternoon wore on, the celebration continued to flourish around Sara, filled with joy and laughter. Yet an invisible wall surrounded her heart. Laughter echoed, and the sounds of joy melded with baby talk and playful banter, but with each passing moment, she felt herself growing more distant—an island of uncertainties in a sea of excitement.

With each game they played, Sara tried desperately to sweep her worries away, wrapping herself in the moment, in the laughter, in the tender sheen of friendship. Yet Victoria continued dropping hints, almost oblivious to the way her words thudded against Sara's heart.

"You're going to be a super mum!" exclaimed Lily, handing over the cutest little onesie that read, *I'm the reason we can't sleep.*

Sara smiled. She loved spending time with her mum's friends, who were starting to feel like her friends too, but she knew they didn't understand how she felt. If she could just scream her love from the rooftops, maybe they would hear it, understand it. But here, in this moment filled with laughter, sugary cakes, and warmth, she could not bring herself to speak the truth.

"I'm really glad all of you are here," she finally managed, her voice laced with sincerity. "You've made this so special."

A chorus of agreement filled the room, heartfelt and genuine. For a moment, Sara allowed herself to sink into it, letting the love and friendship envelop her like a soft blanket. Perhaps, just perhaps, this afternoon could be enough.

Maybe one day, when the time was right, she would find the strength to tell her mum about Charlie. For now, she'd hold on to these delightful moments, the beginning of something beautiful, something real. How could she get them to see? It seemed impossible.

Blog
Comment.
Hey, has there been any new vandalism? When is the best time for stakeout?

Ellie read her one and only comment (disappointed there was only one) and had a good idea who this was from… Amy!

CHAPTER 19: Ellie

While driving across town to meet Lily at the craft store, Ellie could not shake a growing unease. Her fingers drummed nervously against the steering wheel as she replayed the events of the last few weeks in her mind. Since starting her blog, she had seen a steady increase in followers, buoyed by excitement and inspiration. But now, what had once been a reliable source of joy had turned into a troubling enigma. Only one comment and she knew who it was from when normally she would have plenty.

Her numbers had begun to slip, and with each falling statistic, she felt a fragile thread of connection fray. What was happening? She could not quite figure out what had changed. Was it something in the tone of her posts? The topics she chose. Memories of past entries and the joyful comments from her followers echoed in her mind, contrasting sharply with the current silence and dwindling views.

Ellie parked outside the craft store, *Blossom Crafts*, a charming little place absolutely stuffed with supplies. The sign outside was painted in merry hues, each letter carefully hand drawn. Ellie always found comfort in the way the woman who ran it, Gabby, seemed to know everything there was to know about crafting.

Ellie jumped out of her car and glanced around, spotting Lily outside, practically hopping from one foot to the other in impatience. Her fiery hair caught the sunlight as she waved excitedly. When she saw Ellie approaching, her face lit up, a welcome distraction from the dark clouds of worry lingering over Ellie. But Ellie noticed Lily's brow crease with concern a telltale sign that her friend could sense her troubles.

"Hey! You look… up to something." Lily noted, her eyes narrowing playfully.

Ellie laughed, brushing it off with a quick, "I'm fine!" She wasn't about to ruin the day before it even started.

"Shall we head inside?" she suggested, hoping that spending time at the craft store might lift her spirits.

The air inside the hallowed halls of *Blossom Crafts* was rich with the scents of paper, paint, and a hint of something sweet possibly the cookies Gabby often baked. It always felt magical to Ellie, like stepping into another world. They drifted through the aisles, filled to the brim with delightful craft items that sparked inspiration. Each shelf overflowed with vibrant materials, coloured papers in every shade imaginable, and an array of paints that could leave any artist or designer breathless.

"I can't believe how many silk printing supplies I've gone through," Lily said, her eyes gleaming with enthusiasm as she picked up a pack of new silkscreen frames.

"It's just so satisfying! Teddy and I bought a bunch together, but I've used them all up. I think I might be addicted!"

Ellie laughed, her earlier worries momentarily forgotten as Lily animatedly discussed her latest projects. "I'm pretty sure that's a real thing Crafting Addiction," Ellie quipped, grabbing a few rolls of colourful tape.

Lily rolled her eyes, a grin on her face. "What you need is a support group! You can lead it!"

Ellie nodded, feigning seriousness.

"On Tuesdays, we'll meet for tea and tape therapy!" Ellie declared, feeling the heaviness in her chest ease as laughter filled the space around them.

As the giggles subsided, the conversation drifted seamlessly, eventually weaving its way to Amir, Ellie's 'Mystery Man from Dubai.'

"So, what's the latest with Mr. Scrummy?" Lily asked with a playful nudge.

"Oh, Amir is just… he's so romantic and charming," Ellie gushed, her cheeks flushing at the thought of him.

"He has this way with words that is utterly poetic! I cannot believe how well we connect, even across the miles. He sends messages that feel like they could be in a novel."

"Very impressive," Lily replied, her tone teasing.

"You are love struck over a guy from Dubai! That's a unique predicament, I must say."

Ellie laughed, rolling her eyes but feeling warmth in her heart. "I can't help it! He has a way of making the most mundane things sound extraordinary!"

Lily raised an eyebrow. "You know, my brother's name is Amir."

Ellie paused mid-sentence. "Wait, what? *The Amir*?"

"I mean, I don't know. What do you think? Amir is a common name, you know!" Lily replied, laughing.

Ellie remembered a brief encounter with Lily's brother during her stay in Dubai. They had literally collided on a busy street while shopping, but she couldn't quite recall what he looked like.

"Couldn't be the same Amir?" Ellie asked, looking confused.

Their laughter mingled as they turned up the next aisle of the shop, and surprise struck them both like a bolt from the blue. There, hunched over a display of spray paint cans, was none other than… Amy.

"Is that Amy?" Lily whispered, ducking back around the corner, eyes wide with disbelief.

Ellie bit her lip, trying to suppress a giggle. "What on Earth is she doing here? Didn't she tell us she didn't have hobbies?"

"Exactly! Doesn't have time for hobbies with her fancy marketing job!" Lily whispered, eyes darting between the shelves and their unsuspecting friend.

"Yet there she is, flirting with the spray cans," Ellie mused.

"What if Amy is the vandal?" Lily's voice danced on the edge of comedy, but Ellie felt a stirring of doubt.

With a frown, Ellie shook her head. "No way Amy is far too much of a rule follower to be the vandal. But why is she here?"

Suddenly, a light bulb flickered in Ellie's mind as fragments of the last few weeks swirled together. She held a finger to her lips, lowering her voice to a dramatic whisper.

"What if… she's sourcing colours for a project? Maybe a hidden artistic side to Amy?"

Lily gasped theatrically. "An underground artist? That's even better! This is so newsworthy; we could include her in the blog!"

Ellie instantly felt a rush of enthusiasm. "That's brilliant! I'll blog about Amy's secret life!"

As the pair peeked around the corner again, Ellie observed Amy continuing to inspect the array of colourful sprays, her brow furrowed in concentration.

"Well, she looks like she means serious business!" Ellie murmured.

Before they could discuss further, Amy abruptly turned, her gaze scanning the aisle. The girls recoiled, holding their breath as they tried to contain their giggles.

"Let's get a proper look!" Lily whispered as they shifted to a more strategic position.

As if on cue, Amy grabbed a vibrant red can, giving it a shake and turning it over in her hands, brow arching quizzically.

"Maybe she's planning something?" Ellie murmured, grinning.

Lily leaned closer. "What if she's sprucing up our dull old town with her street art? The mystery needs solving! You need to write about it for the blog… 'Amy the Artist'…"

Ellie felt her heart race. Perhaps this was the spark of inspiration she needed. "Yes! It's genius! Exploring the journey of hidden talents, and Amy, the non-hobbyist!"

Just as they debated their plan, Amy turned again, spotting them. A wide smile broke across her face.

"Ellie! Lily! Fancy running into you!"

Ellie plastered on a smile, masking her surprise.

"Hi, Amy! Out picking up supplies, are we?"

"Totally! I've taken up a new hobby!" Amy chimed, a hint of excitement creeping into her voice.

Lily looked back at Ellie, eyes sparkling with mischief.

"That's what we hear! What's this new hobby of yours?"

"Oh, just something fun. Painting! Well, more like a small project I'm considering," Amy replied with a slight laugh, brushing it off but unable to hide the spark in her eyes.

Ellie's heart raced. It seemed Amy had taken an unexpected leap into artistry.

"What are you working on?" she asked, knowing she could weave this into her blog.

"Just a mural in my flat! Nothing too fancy," Amy said, modest but glowing with confidence.

"That's amazing! I'd love to see it!" Lily encouraged warmly.

"Oh, absolutely! You both should come by for a proper reveal. We could make a night of it." Amy said, beaming with pride.

As Amy ambled off with her new spray paints, Ellie turned to Lily, her own spirits lifting significantly.

"Looks like I've got something fun to blog about again! We'll follow Amy's artistic adventure!" Ellie exclaimed, feeling as if a weight had lifted off her shoulders.

"See? I told you this craft store was magical!" Lily replied, giving her a playful nudge.

As they roamed the aisles, discussing project ideas and designer dreams, Ellie felt the embers of her creativity ignite once more. Suddenly, an idea struck her—how to bring back her followers without divulging her friends' secrets.

As they left the store, their baskets filled with a vibrant array of supplies, Ellie felt invigorated. Inspired by both Amir and Amy, she was eager to reconnect with her followers, weaving together tales of laughter, creativity, and a hint of mystery. With a beaming smile, she glanced around at the bright autumn sky above, sensing the thrill of possibilities unfurling before her while.

A thought suddenly struck her like a bolt from the blue.

"What if Amy is in love with the vandal?" she said to Lily.

Lily screamed with delight.

"Amy wants to find a way to meet up with Noah again. She's thinking of 'vandalizing' the shop to get Noah to come and clean them. Brilliant! We must tell Jess!"

Ellie pulled out her phone but stopped. She couldn't. She had promised no more sharing secrets.

Lily tried to convince her, but Ellie held firm. Amy was on her own; she would reach out if she needed help getting Noah's attention.

As they headed home, laughter bounced between them, and Ellie realised that sometimes a little adventure was all it took to reignite her creative spark.

Email from Dubai:
From: A.J.
To: Ellie Edwards
Subject: Worried!!
Hey Ellie, you don't quite sound like yourself. Is everything okay? Amir

From: Ellie Edwards
To: A.J.
Subject: Re: Worried!
You are right Amir. I just feel I keep being too honest... for all the right reasons but feel I am getting into trouble getting too involved and sharing secrets.

From: A.J.
To: Ellie Edwards
Subject: Worried!!
But Ellie, that is exactly the reason I fell in love with you, along with your passport photograph. I love your honesty.
Amir x

From: Ellie Edwards
To: A.J.
Subject: Re: Worried!
Wait, you love me??

CHAPTER 20: **Amy**

Amy was never particularly excited about any of the events at Shoperapy. The stakeout had been mildly entertaining, even if they hadn't caught the vandal that night. This event, however, was something she was actively dreading Jess's bridal dress shopping.

The thought of spending an afternoon surrounded by frills, lace, and heartfelt sighs filled her with an anxiety she couldn't quite shake. Steeling her nerves, Amy entered Shoperapy with dramatic resolve, as if she were walking into a lion's den. She promised herself she wouldn't scowl too much.

"Just a smile, that's all," she murmured under her breath, feeling ridiculous even saying it aloud.

After all, it wasn't Jess's fault that Amy believed love, and particularly marriage was torture. With her heart heavy, she reasoned that Jess was either about to learn that hard lesson or prove Amy wrong. Either way, Amy didn't want to rain on her friend's parade; life had a way of doing that without her help.

As she stepped inside, Amy immediately felt the unique atmosphere of Shoperapy. The space buzzed with electric anticipation. The air was thick with optimistic chatter and giddy laughter, and the dresses hanging from the ceiling swayed gently, like swans gliding across a lake. Grace was busy arranging wedding gowns specially ordered for Jess, each one more extravagant than the last, straight out of a fairy tale.

Amy knew she wished she could feel that magic too. Being surrounded by so much enthusiasm only intensified the dark cloud swirling in her own heart.

She sighed as she settled onto a plush couch in the corner, feeling painfully out of place amid the joyous atmosphere of Shoperapy. As she tentatively sipped a glass of champagne hoping it might offer some comfort, her thoughts drifted, uninvited, to the spectre of her past. How had she ended up here, sitting at a bridal fitting when she'd once envisioned an entirely different life where she was the bride?

In the back room, Ellie and Grace bustled around Jess, helping her into the first dress, while Amy grew increasingly lost in thought, memories flooding her mind.

Her reflection stared back at her from a nearby mirror as she shifted in her seat. She looked unmistakably unhappy, though moments earlier she hadn't thought herself to be. The black suit she wore appeared harsh against the surrounding vibrant colours, as though she'd dressed for the role of a cynical critic in a play. Smiling felt like squeezing into shoes two sizes too small, uncomfortable, and restrictive, making her acutely aware of how low her spirits truly were.

This moment in Shoperapy was nothing like what she'd imagined for her life, even as a young girl dreaming of her own perfect wedding. Instead, she felt like a spectator in her own sad story, watching others step into happiness while she remained locked outside its circle in misery.

When Jess finally emerged from the fitting room, the contrast was impossible to ignore.

She floated out in an ethereal embroidered gown, a tiara perched like a sparkling crown on top of her head, radiating happiness from every pore. Ellie and Grace erupted with oohs and aahs, their faces alight as they mirrored Jess's joy.

"Oh, my goodness, Jess! You look like an absolute princess!" Ellie exclaimed, her enthusiasm unmistakable.

For a brief moment, Amy almost felt happy too. It was impossible not to be touched by Ellie's excitement. But then a darker realisation settled over her like a heavy storm cloud, suffocating her once again.

She had to admit it to herself: Jess, standing there in that dress, radiated life, happiness, and hope. She embodied everything bright and beautiful, everything Amy felt she had lost. The contrast tightened around Amy's heart, squeezing until she could barely breathe.

"Doesn't it make you feel even slightly silly?" Amy muttered dryly, arching an eyebrow at Jess with an exaggerated huff, half-hoping to provoke a reaction.

Jess's response was immediate a playful punch to Amy's arm followed by a full-bodied laugh.

"You're just being a drama queen! How could I feel even a little silly? I feel beautiful… like a real bride." Jess laughed, spinning to admire herself in the tall mirror across the room.

"Oh, don't be silly, Amy!" she continued, beaming as her fingers brushed the fabric of her gown, as though it were spun from pure happiness.

"It's just a dress! Look at how it twirls! You could join in the fun, you know. One of these could be hanging in your wardrobe someday too!"

Amy watched as Jess' heart soared, unburdened by reality. A sharp pang twisted in her chest with every joyful proclamation Jess made. She longed for even a flicker of that happiness, yet felt rooted firmly in the past, a prisoner of her own memories.

Out loud, though, Amy pointed out everything she disliked, a hint of bitterness slipping into her voice.

"It's just flouncy tulle and expensive material," she said with a dismissive wave of her hand.

"You might want to reconsider this whole romantic notion before making any lifelong commitments."

Her tone dripped with sarcasm, but inside she was battling a whirlpool of emotion a tangled mix of affection and resentment that tore at her from within.

Jess merely rolled her eyes, unfazed, turning back to the mirror. She was far too excited to be derailed by Amy's commentary. Grace smiled on, bright-eyed and determined to keep the mood light, even as Amy shot her a pointed glance.

"Well, not every dress looks good on everyone," Amy added mischievously, crossing her arms. "That one seems a bit… erm fluffy."

"Fluffy?" Jess gasped, clutching her chest in mock horror as though Amy had committed a cardinal fashion sin. The atmosphere wavered slightly, Jess's excitement pausing just long enough to respond.

"It's fabulous! Honestly, Amy, if you weren't such a misery, you might actually enjoy this. It's like something straight out of a fairy tale."

"Fairy tales are for people who enjoy living in la-la land, darling,"

Amy shot back with a teasing smirk, their not so friendly banter continuing.

Still, tucked away in a quiet corner of her heart, Amy felt a flicker of pride for Jess. Her smile so genuine, so alive was difficult to resist entirely.

As Jess tried on gown after gown, each more extravagant than the last, Amy found herself growing increasingly nitpicky, her cynicism sharpening with every passing moment, as though negativity were the only shield she had left.

"Oh, come now, that one makes you look a bit like a custard pudding," Amy scoffed, earning a loud laugh from Grace and a playful punch from Jess.

"A custard pudding?" Grace wheezed, dramatically clutching her chest. "Now *that's* original, Amy! I'm sure that was exactly the designer's vision when they made that gown!"

With a sharp tongue and quicker wit, Amy shot back with a sarcastic glare.

"I aim to please, obviously."

"Okay, Amy, how about *you* try one on?" Jess suggested, her enthusiasm making Amy's heart flutter for all the wrong reasons. The mere thought of being zipped into a wedding dress nearly made Amy choke on her champagne.

"Me? In one of those things?" she gasped theatrically. "I'd have to charge admission. Trust me nobody's ready for that visual!"

Jess threw her head back, laughing so hard it felt as though they were back at school again, carefree and unburdened by adult disappointments.

The laughter that followed was genuinely uplifting even for Amy, who felt the faintest tug of happiness at being part of it. But pity and nostalgia crept in like uninvited guests, slipping through the cracks of her humour and filling her chest with memories she'd rather keep buried. She couldn't help but imagine herself in dresses just like these. Back then, the future had sparkled with promise. Now, those dreams tasted bitter.

Matthew.

The thought of him sent a chill straight down her spine, freezing her insides despite the warmth of Jess's excitement. He had chosen ambition over love, let success crush something fragile and precious between them. As Jess admired herself in layers of lace and tulle, Amy felt betrayal rise in her throat like bile. With every twirl, the memories surged higher, threatening to pull her under. The smiles around her felt cruel, magnifying her heartache in a room charged with joy.

"Maybe you should consider something sleeker?" Amy suggested as Jess emerged in an impossibly intricate lace gown, her tone brittle despite herself.

"Sleeker?" Jess repeated, incredulous. "I'm getting married not heading to a board meeting!" She laughed, green eyes shining.

"I'm just saying less fluff, more sophistication," Amy quipped, her voice sharp enough to sting. Even as she spoke, the weight of her words pressed heavily on her chest.

Jess studied her reflection, her brow creasing slightly, her excitement dimming just a fraction.

"It's just... not my style," Amy continued, irritation and blind anguish bleeding through.

"What do they even think when they design these things?"

Finally, with a deep breath of resignation, Jess clenched her fists briefly, absorbing the blow of Amy's comments. Then she took a breath, stepped out of the gown, and faced Amy with quiet resolve.

"You know," she said gently, "it's okay to feel what you're feeling. But don't you see how beautiful this moment can be even if you can't feel it yourself?"

Amy bit her lip, painfully aware of how she must look amid all the joy and chaos. Jess's sympathy wrapped around her, heavy and sincere, reminding her of the affection that bound them together.

"It's just hard," Amy murmured. "You're all"

"Glowing?" Grace cut in, mischief sparkling in her eyes as she wielded humour like a perfectly timed lifeline.

Amy snorted despite herself, irritation colliding with affection.

"Oh, good grief I'm not about to burst into flames!"

The three of them burst into laughter, and for that brief moment, the weight on Amy's heart lifted just enough to breathe. Friendship, imperfect and unfiltered, wrapped around her like a fragile but welcome shield.

At last, Amy couldn't keep the chuckle at bay as Jess enthusiastically slipped into yet another gown, her joyful energy impossible to resist. The contrast between them was stark, yet in that moment, Amy found a sliver of clarity amid the swirl of emotion. Even if she was still trapped in the past, drowning in old memories, she knew deep down that Jess deserved this day, this moment of unfiltered happiness.

"Alright, alright," Amy conceded, a reluctant smile breaking through her stony façade.

"I'll be nice. I promise not to compare every dress to an overly critical board meeting."

She gestured towards Jess, her tone softening.

"Let's just find a dress that makes you feel like the gorgeous bride you're going to be."

Jess's joy radiated freely, uncontained, and something in Amy's chest ached to feel even a fraction of that warmth.

As Jess twirled again, graceful as a ballet dancer, Amy felt a flicker ignite inside her small, fragile, heart as laughter bubbled around them, weaving itself into the air, and at that moment Amy was reminded of the quiet magic of friendship and love. Maybe, just maybe, there was still happiness waiting for her too, even if it arrived in unexpected forms… even if it came wrapped in taffeta and lace. Even if she couldn't embrace marriage, she could celebrate Jess.

"You're coming around, Amy! You really are!" Jess declared, spinning once more before flashing a radiant, hopeful smile.

"Don't push it," Amy replied, rolling her eyes, though she couldn't quite hide her laughter.

"I still think marriage is madness."

"Then at least it's *beautiful* madness," Jess shot back, her laughter ringing through the room and blending with the happiness of her friends.

Surrounded by silk, laughter, and love, Amy began to feel not just bitterness but warmth. A painful, tender warmth that reminded her that love, like the gowns hanging all around them, was layered, complicated, and still capable of shining even in the darkest corners. Despite her cynicism, she realised that perhaps Jess and Adam *were* doing the right thing, and that realisation made her want to cry.

She excused herself abruptly. She had been halfway through criticising yet another dress when it hit her, she *loved* it. It was perfect. And that shattered her, because once, not so long ago, that moment could have been hers.

As she fled Shoperapy, Ellie called after her, but Amy didn't stop. She ran as if her life depended on it.

Outside, the tears finally spilled as she reached her car, breathless and broken. The joy, the laughter, the gowns it was all too much.

She never wanted to set foot in Shoperapy again or hear anything more about Jess and Adam's wedding.

CHAPTER 21: **Lily**

Lily ran down the street as if she were being chased, her feet pounding against the pavement faster than she'd ever thought possible. She weaved through tourists and shoppers, brushing past bags stuffed with shopping and snacks. Her hairclip slipped from the top of her head and clattered to the ground behind her but there was no time to turn back. She would have to go without it.

The unusually warm autumn sun shone overhead, casting a harsh light that beaded sweat on her brow, mixing with the heat of her racing heart. Any concern about looking dishevelled vanished as adrenaline surged through her veins, propelling her forward.

She darted into Shoperapy, the familiar jingle of the doorbell ringing out behind her. Breathless and flushed, Lily stumbled inside, her heart hammering like a drum. Ellie, perched behind the checkout counter with her hair pulled into a messy bun, looked up instantly, alarm flashing across her face.

"Lily what's wrong?!" she exclaimed, confusion melting quickly into concern.

"I need you to hide me and hide me *quick*!" Lily gasped, her voice dropping to a frantic whisper as she glanced over her shoulder, as though a dragon were stalking her, ready to scorch her world with confrontation and unwanted truths.

There wasn't time to explain. Lily was grateful Ellie didn't waste a second on questions. She sprang into action, grabbing a handful of multicoloured scarves and tossing them onto a nearby rack while motioning for Lily to follow her towards the back of the shop. The scarves fluttered through the air, bright splashes of colour against the boutique's muted walls.

"Come on quick!" Ellie whispered urgently, casting a wary glance towards the door as she guided Lily into the dressing rooms.

The dressing rooms were decorated with large, absurd mirrors framed in vibrant pink, their reflections amplifying the anxiety that filled the space. The scent of incense mingled with the chatter of shoppers buying a new outfit outside, creating a cocoon of familiarity amid the whirlwind of Lily's mixed emotions. Just as they stepped inside, Ellie barely managed to ask…

"Who exactly are you hiding from?"

"Teddy!" Lily blurted out.

Her eyes widened with curiosity, a mixture of concern and playful curiosity lingering in them.

At that moment, the bell above the door tinkled again. Panic jolted through her. Lily instinctively slipped behind a curtain, peeking through a narrow gap just in time to see Teddy walk in, scanning the shop with those strikingly sincere eyes.

"Can I help you, Teddy?" Ellie's voice turned bright and cheerful as she stepped forward, positioning herself perfectly to block his view of the dressing rooms.

Ellie's voice turned bright and cheerful as she stepped forward, positioning herself to perfectly block Teddy's sight of her friend.

"Uh… yeah," he replied, surprise lacing his tone as his brow furrowed with concern.

"I'm supposed to meet Lily here for our date."

He hesitated, then added softly,

"We were going to explore the Castle today."

The words hung in the air. A bittersweet reminder of plans made, and feelings Lily wasn't quite ready to face.

Ellie feigned a sympathetic smile, her eyes twinkling with mischief as she softened her voice.

"Oh, I'm really sorry, but Lily isn't here right now."

Her tone edged towards playful, creating a protective shield around Lily's racing heart.

Lily winced at the surprise in Teddy's voice, a wave of regret washing over her like cold water.

"Oh… really? Do you know when she'll be back?" His brow creased with sincerity, and the concern in his voice sent another stab of guilt straight through Lily's chest.

"She'll be here soon, I'm sure," Ellie assured him, catching Lily's anxiety-filled gaze. She raised an eyebrow at her friend—a silent but unmistakable message: *You'd better come out soon.*

"She had something special she wanted to pick up for your date, and she didn't want to spoil the surprise!"

Lily's insides twisted painfully. She knew she should step out and tell him the truth, but the thought of facing him felt utterly overwhelming. The weight of everything left unsaid pressed down on her shoulders, as though she were sinking into quicksand.

"What kind of something?" Teddy asked, scratching his head. Curiosity mingled with patience in his expression, his sweetness making Lily's heart ache.

"Uh… it's a surprise!" Ellie replied smoothly, charmingly deflecting the question.

"You know how Lily is about surprises. She's just checking on it, that's all."

The ease of Ellie's answer steadied the air, holding Lily's indecision at bay.

The exchange stirred memories of all the plans Lily and Teddy had made together outings that once brimmed with excitement, now feeling like echoes of something slipping just out of reach.

Ellie glanced back towards the dressing rooms and raised her voice to keep the ruse alive.

"Ms. Hamilton, are you sure you don't want to come out?"

Lily inhaled sharply, pitching her voice into an exaggerated tone to disguise her panic.

"No, no! You'd better bring me some different options. None of these are going to work!"

Conviction tinged her words, even if they were nothing more than a cover.

Lily's heart thundered in her ears, the noise of the shop fading into a distant hum as her phone buzzed in her pocket. Teddy's name flashed across the screen like an alarm bell. Her stomach twisted as she silenced it, praying he hadn't noticed.

Lily could almost hear her heart thumping in her ears, the noise of the bustling shop fading into a muffled echo as her phone buzzed in her pocket, ringing with Teddy's name flashing across the screen like an alarm bell. She needed to silence it before he could see; her stomach twisted uncomfortably in response. As much as she wished she could simply join him outside and everything would return to normal, she knew she could not face him at this moment.

Time stretched unbearably, every second thick with tension. Eventually, she heard Teddy ask Ellie if she could call him when Lily arrived.

"I'm sure she has a good excuse for missing our date," he said, hope threading through his voice. "I'll come right back if you let me know."

Lily's heart sank. She had never meant to hurt him, but the looming pulls of Dubai felt like a black hole inescapable, threatening to swallow everything she cared about. While she hid, he stood outside, waiting, believing.

When the door finally closed behind Teddy, Ellie swept aside the curtain, arms crossed, eyebrows raised. The dressing room felt suddenly heavy with expectation.

"Talk."

Lily's cheeks burned crimson as embarrassment flooded in.

"I panicked," she whispered.

"Teddy and I agreed the Castle would be the last stop before I leave. It means... it's the end of my time here. I'll be going home."

Her voice trembled, caught between resignation and doubt.

"Then why are you hiding?" Ellie pressed gently but firmly. "You should just tell him."

Lily hesitated, her thoughts knotted and tangled. The truth was complicated.

She now wasn't sure she wanted to go back to Dubai at all.

"Every moment I avoid facing him is another moment I can pretend I'm not leaving," Lily confessed, her voice shrinking, as if afraid her words might collapse under their own weight.

It sounded foolish, almost childish, yet part of her honestly believed that if she never went to the Castle with Teddy, her departure date might simply dissolve—lost to time, forgotten entirely.

"I know I'm being ridiculous," she sighed, her breath hitching as tears gathered in her eyes.

"Maybe if I keep avoiding it, it won't have to happen. I wish I could just… wish it all away."

The words lingered between them, heavy and unresolved.

Ellie rolled her eyes, a soft laugh escaping her, though the warmth in her gaze betrayed how deeply she understood.

"Lily, avoidance has never worked for anyone," she said gently but firmly. "You can't keep hiding. You have to face it."

Her words were firm yet caring, a testament to their friendship.

When panic flickered across Lily's face, Ellie's tone softened.

"Hey. We'll figure something out. We always do. Look at everything we've survived so far, we've faced it together. This is no different."

Her reassurance wrapped around Lily like a familiar blanket.

Grateful, Lily managed a weak smile, though the weight on her chest still felt crushing.

"Thanks, Ellie," she mumbled, biting her lip in contemplation, her thoughts a wild tempest.

After a brief silence, Ellie brightened deliberately.

"Just think about it today could be beautiful. The Castle might surprise you. You might even love it… and not want to leave at all."

A small laugh escaped Lily, fleeting but real.

"Maybe. But right now, I just want to breathe and pretend everything else doesn't exist."

"Okay," Ellie said calmly. "Deep breaths. In… and out…"

She counted softly as they breathed together, the tension slowly loosening its grip.

"Now what?" Lily asked, feeling lighter but still uncertain, the truth hovering like thick fog.

"You tell Teddy the truth," Ellie replied, her voice steady. "You can do this."

Lily nodded, a spark of resolve igniting beneath her fear.

"Okay… you're right. I can do this," she said quietly.

She knew she had to talk to Teddy. She was still terrified, but she knew what she had to do.

As Lily gathered the courage to take a risk, Ellie felt something shift inside herself too. Watching her friend hide behind fear made one thing painfully clear:

She couldn't keep doing the same.

Ellie pulled out her phone and began to type.

From: Ellie Edwards
To: A.J.
Subject: Secrets
Hi Amir,
I'm done trying to be reserved after seeing how keeping secrets and not telling someone how you feel about them can stop you from meeting the one, which is why I am hosting a Secrets Night and why I want to share my secret with you…
I love talking to you and I want to meet you. That's my secret!
Ellie xx

Secrets Night @Shoperapy

Tuesday @ 8pm

Join us for a not so hush-hush night. As always, there will be bubbles, clothes, and chat.

See you all there,

Ellie xx

CHAPTER 22: Sara

Sara and Victoria arrived together at Shoperapy just as twilight settled in. The sign above the entrance sparkled softly, its glow hinting at excitement and mystery behind the heavy velvet drapes that obscured the windows. Sara felt the familiar knot tighten in her stomach.

Her secret the one she had been carrying quietly was beginning to feel heavier by the day. The phrase *Secrets Night* echoed uncomfortably in her mind. What did it really mean? And what, exactly, might it demand of her?

For a fleeting moment, she considered inventing an excuse to stay home. Morning sickness perhaps or some vague, pregnancy-related ailment that no one would question. But curiosity won out. It always did. And besides, Shoperapy had become more than just a boutique, it was a place of warmth, connection, and friendship.

Lately, Sara had found herself leaning into that sense of community more than ever. She knew she would need it when she finally told her mum the truth about Charlie and how she had fallen for him in a big way and that she believed he was the one. The thought alone sent a shiver through her heart.

Would they judge her? Would they understand?

Charlie had wanted to tell Victoria and her dad weeks ago. He was bursting with excitement, proud of their relationship, eager to stop pretending. But Sara had insisted on waiting. Holding the secret gave her a sense of control, as though timing alone could soften the impact.

She told herself there would be a perfect moment. A magical hour when the words would come easily and everything would fall into place.

But as she stood in front of Shoperapy glowing entrance, anxiety crept in. What if that moment never came? What if waiting only made things worse?

With a shared, unspoken apprehension, Sara and Victoria stepped inside.

The shift in atmosphere was immediate. Soft music played in the background, and the air was warm with the scent of scented candles. The boutique looked beautiful colourful clothing arranged artfully on racks, accessories catching the light, cheerful potted plants scattered throughout the space. It felt intimate, comforting. Like a hug.

Ellie stood near the entrance, drink in hand, greeting guests with her signature warmth. She looked radiant confident, joyful, completely at ease. It was impossible not to be drawn in by her energy.

"Bubbles for you, Victoria!" Ellie announced, handing her a flute fizzing with effervescence.

"And a delightful non-alcoholic concoction for you, Sara, of course."

Sara smiled, genuinely grateful. Ellie never missed the minute details. She always made sure everyone felt included never singled out, never awkward. It was one of the many reasons people loved her.

"Thank you, Ellie!" Victoria said brightly, already buzzing with excitement.

"So," she added, leaning in conspiratorially. "What do you have planned for us tonight?"

Ellie had a talent for turning ordinary evenings into something memorable. As Sara glanced around the room, her curiosity deepened. Maybe tonight would bring clarity. Maybe it would give her the courage she'd been lacking.

Ellie's lips curved into a slow, knowing smirk.

The kind that promised secrets wouldn't stay hidden for long.

A knowing glimmer flickered in Ellie's eye as she beckoned them deeper into the shop. The excitement in the air felt charged, humming with possibility, and despite her nerves, Sara felt a spark ignite inside her. The thrill of the unknown tugged at her curiosity, refusing to be ignored.

Sara raised an eyebrow, amused by Ellie's unmistakable flair for drama. It wasn't unusual for her to turn an event into a spectacle, but tonight felt different, electric, almost intentional. As Ellie reached the centre of the boutique, she dramatically shrugged off her trench coat with a flourish. What she revealed stopped them in their tracks.

Over her chic outfit, Ellie wore her undergarments on the outside… black bras with intricate detailing layered boldly over her clothes. The look was audacious, unapologetic, and utterly Ellie. Sara and Victoria burst into laughter, quickly joined by the other friends, the sound filling the boutique with warmth and disbelief.

"What *is* this?" Sara laughed, shaking her head in delight.

"Is this what you meant by taking risks?"

The laughter rippled through the room, contagious and freeing.

"I thought you said tonight was about secrets!" Sara teased, still grinning at the spectacle.

There was something wildly liberating about Ellie's defiance of convention. The boldness of it all stirred something deeper in Sara a quiet recognition that maybe this night wasn't just about confessions.

Maybe it was about authenticity. About owning who you are, even when it feels uncomfortable.

Ellie laughed, a full, joyful sound that lifted the mood instantly.

"Oh, that will come later," she said playfully.

"But it wouldn't be a night at Shoperapy without a little fashion and it's time we all took some much-needed risks. Fashion should be fun and expressive."

She shot Sara a sly wink, and something fluttered unsteadily in Sara's chest. A mix of laughter, embarrassment, and a strange flicker of courage.

Soon, more woman arrived, the boutique filled with excited greetings and playful banter. Ellie wasted no time, encouraging everyone to experiment to layer, to clash, to break the rules. Black and red bras were worn over crisp white shirts, garters draped over silk trousers, combinations so unexpected they hovered between ridiculous and stunning.

The room buzzed with laughter as everyone admired one another, unsure whether they looked absurd or astonishingly fabulous. Everyone was caught in a delightful conundrum, unsure whether they looked ridiculous or astonishingly fabulous.

"That is fashion for you! And I would say, you all look fabulous."

Ellie declared, surveying the electrifying chaos with pride shining in her eyes.

It felt like a collective release, a moment where risk-taking wasn't just allowed, but celebrated. The atmosphere softened as everyone settled onto plush cushions scattered around the boutique, cocktails, and snacks in hand.

As the chatter quietened, Ellie clasped her hands together. Her tone shifted still warm, but unmistakably serious.

"I know there have been secrets," she said gently.

"Rumours. Feelings kept hidden."

The room stilled.

"And I think it might be time to bring our insides out," she continued.

"So… who would like to share something tonight?"

Sara shifted uncomfortably in her seat, her thoughts racing. Did Ellie mean for *her* to speak up? A quick glance around the room revealed quiet nods of encouragement from the other women Lily, Jess, even Amy, who was rarely one to open up. The tension was palpable, like a tightrope stretched over a chasm, daring someone to take the first step. This evening felt like an invitation to step beyond comfort zones, to lower defences, and to be vulnerable together.

Ellie's voice cut gently through the moment, steady and reassuring.

"I've had my own struggles with how best to handle all of this," she said. "For a long time, I tried not sharing, keeping everything bottled up, staying quiet. But I realised that helps no one. Telling the truth to the people we love may be uncomfortable at first, but in the end, it's always better. We need to take more risks, especially with love."

There was a quiet wisdom in her words, and Sara felt them settle deep within her. Maybe this *was* the moment not just for the sake of others, but for herself too.

Ellie opened the floor, and for a few heavy seconds, silence followed. The air thickened with apprehension. Then Ellie smiled and broke it herself.

"Well, I suppose I'll go first. I've been talking to a mystery man from Dubai and I really like him."

What could have felt exposing, instead felt light, even joyful.

After her revelation, others began to speak up, sharing their own secrets in hushed tones that grew louder with every word, encouragement rippling through the group. Sara felt her anxiety ebbing away, observing how supportive everyone was during this cathartic moment. It was inspiring, witnessing the release of pent-up emotions among women who had previously hid their truths as they feared being ridiculed but the laughter of their friends turned into heartfelt conversations of support.

As the discussions continued, Ellie smiled at Sara knowingly, and Sara felt a strange surge of courage blossoming within her. Perhaps tonight, just maybe, would mark the beginning of their collective empowerment, a night where secrets could transform from feelings of anxiety into pillars of strength and understanding. She could feel the warmth of camaraderie enveloping her, and she knew deep inside that the time had come for her to join in.

"I guess I have a secret too," Sara finally said, her voice trembling slightly as the eyes of the room turned towards her.

"I've been seeing someone too and I'm in love with him."

The confession hung in the air, palpable, as she awaited the reactions. To her surprise, a wave of encouragement washed over her, not the judgment she feared. Victoria's eyes widened with excitement. Was Sara finally going to reveal who she was seeing?

As her friends rallied around her with supportive words and stories of their own, the energy in the room felt electric. In that moment, under the warm light of Shoperapy, Sara realised that sharing her truth, or part of it had lifted a weight off her shoulders. She looked around at her friends, at the faces filled with understanding and empathy, and felt an overwhelming sense of gratitude. Tonight, had truly transformed from a night of secrets into a celebration of honesty and friendship, a collective release of their vulnerabilities that allowed them all to embrace who they were and what they wanted, or who!

As the night wore on, laughter and stories flowed freely, bridges forming where gaps had once seemed too wide to cross. This wasn't just a gathering it was sisterhood, forged in truth. The atmosphere shimmered with connection, and Sara felt a bond forming with each woman present, knowing that secrets would no longer isolate them but rather unite them. It wasn't just about revealing hidden truths, it was about discovering the strength in vulnerability, and at that moment, everything felt right. Sara felt this was more than a gathering; it was a celebration of sisterhood, forged in honesty, courage, and love.

When her mum asked, Sara was about to share the name of the man she was in love with, but at the last minute she just could not do it and was glad of the distraction of her mum's phone ringing…

CHAPTER 23: **Amy**

Amy was sprawled on the couch in her cosy flat, the soft glow of her laptop casting a pale halo across her face. It was Friday night the long-awaited end of the week and yet here she was, tapping away at another dull assignment. This had become her routine: work, Netflix, takeaway, repeat. Once, she'd found comfort in the predictability.

Although it was all predictable, and there was comfort in that, for some reason, this Friday felt different. A peculiar heaviness settled within her, like a cloud looming above and blocking out the warmth of her previous contentment.

Amy felt the nagging feeling of loneliness creeping in and found herself blaming the people she had recently met through Adam and Jess. But most of all, she knew it was Noah who was making tonight feel lonely. Oh, Noah! From their fateful meeting during an unforgettable night. He had stirred feelings in her that were at once thrilling and terrifying. That connection felt electric, stirring possibilities barely waiting to be ignited. Yet, somehow, all of them had seemed to drift away like autumn leaves swept up in a gust of wind, leaving Amy adrift, feeling utterly isolated and, perhaps, a bit broken.

As if to punctuate her thoughts, a sharp knock pierced through the hushed atmosphere of her flat, reverberating in the stillness and pulling her from her doomed spiral of loneliness.

Visitors were rare, almost unheard of. Her social circle had shrunk to near nonexistence, aside from the tentative friendships she'd formed with the women from Shoperapy, relationships she still wasn't sure how to label. The idea of someone standing at her door felt both thrilling and unsettling.

She hesitated, hand hovering mid-air. What if she didn't answer?

Curiosity won.

Taking a steadying breath, she opened the door to find Jess standing there, hair bouncing with barely contained excitement, bright blue eyes glittering with mischief under the glow of the streetlamp. Jess looked like pure momentum alive with energy, possibility spilling from every inch of her.

"Amy! Let's do something *wild* tonight!" Jess announced, already stepping inside without waiting for permission.

Amy raised an eyebrow, irritation flickering through her exhaustion.

"Isn't it a bit late for a coffee catch-up?" she muttered, shutting the door behind her. She had zero interest in the usual rituals of coffee, wine, or heaven forbid, beer. They felt tired, predictable, and entirely unappealing.

"Nope. Absolutely not," Jess said, shaking her head with dramatic conviction.

"No coffee. No wine. No beer."

"Nope! We are not doing the standard coffee or wine or beer,"

Jess shook her head vigorously, feigning absolute conviction as if she had declared a war on normalcy.

"There will need to be very little talking anyway, and it will not take long. Just trust me."

She grinned.

Amy sighed, already sensing that her quiet Friday night was officially over.

Amy raised an eyebrow, scepticism jangling like wind chimes in a storm. She had no idea what Jess had planned, but the sparkle in her friend's eyes was both enchanting and alarming, stirring a mix of trepidation and intrigue within her.

Before she could protest, Jess grabbed her arm and pulled her out of the flat, brandishing a brightly coloured plastic bag. Inside, the clink of spray cans hinted at chaos a rainbow of potential mischief packed tightly together.

"Wait, Jess what on Earth are you doing?" Amy gasped, her eyes widening in disbelief as the implications of Jess' intentions settled uncomfortably in her mind.

"Come on! I've got black ski masks for both of us in the car," Jess said, practically vibrating with excitement.

"We're going to make a statement!"

Amy froze. "Make a statement? But…"

Words failed her. Panic and exhilaration churned together, making her pulse pound. This felt reckless, the kind of audacious nonsense that might get their names whispered about in scandalized tones tomorrow. And yet… a spark of thrill flickered inside her. Could she really let go, just this once?

As they snuck towards Shoperapy, the night air carried a heady blend of rebellion and anxiety, swirling around them like mist. Amy glanced sideways at Jess, who practically glowed with mischief. For the first time in ages, Amy felt a surge of potential brimming inside her, a tempting invitation to let her hair down and simply be.

She was swept away by the whirlpool of Jess's energy, and for the first time in ages, Amy felt a rush of potential brimming over inside; could she really let her hair down?

"What if Noah comes out to clean up the spray paint?" Amy whispered, palms clammy, stomach twisting.

"Who cares?" Jess whispered back, barely stifling a giggle. "Let's have some fun! He won't even see us."

The sheer recklessness of the moment began to empower Amy, energising her passing thoughts of modesty and caution. Some part of her relished the defiance, feeling alive in a way she hadn't for far too long. The knots in her stomach loosened just a little as they passed under flickering streetlights, which seemed to cast judgmental glances at their audacity.

They arrived at the side of the building, hiding behind a bush that provided cover against any potential onlookers.

"Okay, you hold this," Jess declared, handing Amy a can of vibrant pink spray paint with an energising flourish.

"And I'll take this one." Anxiety mingled with anticipation as they prepared their tools of mayhem. The thrill of artistic rebellion washed over them like waves crashing against a shore, a total defiance of the ordinary.

"What exactly are we tagging?"

Amy asked, exhilaration and nerves coiling together as she examined the can in her hand. The graffiti felt more than an act of rebellion; it was a canvas for their untamed emotions, the raw feelings she had locked away far too long.

"A masterpiece!" Jess declared, eyes sparkling with wild ambition.

"What else would you expect from two daring artists? Something that captures our glorious night of rebellion. Something that embodies our freedom!"

With a flurry of excitement, they sprayed wild swirls of colour across the windows of Shoperapy. Their designs were a chaotic riot, showcasing their disregard for rules while injecting vibrancy into the drab landscape. The cans hissed and spat, leaving bright trails of colour that challenged the ordinary, each stroke more exhilarating than the last.

But as their laughter echoed, a beam of yellow light cut through the darkness like a spotlight, illuminating their chaotic artwork and casting long shadows on the ground. An authoritative voice boomed, sharp and unforgiving:

"FREEZE!"

Amy and Jess locked eyes in alarm, shock flashing across their faces as the weight of the moment settled in. Dread pooled in their stomachs. Instinctively, they raised their hands, hearts hammering as panic gripped them. This was not how the adventure was supposed to go. Jess thought, as they stood there, bathed in the harsh light, a swirling mix of regret and adrenaline clouding her thoughts, each second stretching unbearably.

Eventually, they found themselves sitting side by side on a wooden bench in the police station, a world away from the spontaneity of their night. The bustling noise, ringing phones, and chatter of officers felt surreal, almost drowning out the harsh reality as their information was processed. Jess fidgeted, biting her lip, fingers trembling as if trying to dispel their predicament.

"Amy, I'm really sorry I got you arrested…"

The guilt in her voice weighed heavily, her eyes searching Amy's for a hint of forgiveness. There was a vulnerability in Jess that Amy recognised; she could sense her friend's fear gnawing at her.

Amy wanted to reassure her, and forced a strained smile, turning to Jess with steady composure.

"Honestly, unbelievably, I'm actually having so much fun and I'm also really happy that you are marrying Adam. You will make a great sister-in-law."

The comment flowed freely, a sincere brightening twist midst the sobering atmosphere brought by the police car.

The mention of Adam caught Jess off guard, prompting a tentative smile to emerge on her face, a mixture of relief and gratitude washing over her.

"Thanks, Amy! I needed to hear that, especially now," she replied, nudging Amy gently with her shoulder.

Their banter began to peel away some of the tension that had settled in the space between them; it felt like shared resolve midst the uncertainty of their predicament.

In that moment of vulnerability, the two women leaned their heads against one another, finding solace in their friendship as the world rattled along around them. Despite the overwhelming circumstances, this shared experience deliberately forced them to confront their relationship and bond more deeply in their shared mischief. Time seemed to pass slowly, each second stretching into eternity as they sat together in suspense, their minds racing with thoughts of what would happen next. But within that shared silence, a resolution began to crystallise between them. Each heartbeat echoed with the certainty that they were not in this alone; the oppressive weight of their predicament began to lift as laughter flickered through the air.

As they shared quiet chuckles, a spark reignited between them; they were partners in mischief, and partners in this unexpected adventure. In the cold, stark light of the police station, their friendship glowed brighter than ever, a reminder that even in moments like these, bonds forged were unbreakable, grounded in understanding and support. So many questions swirled within Amy's thoughts: What did tomorrow hold? How would they laugh this off tomorrow in hindsight? But for tonight, all she needed was Jess's presence, that warmth and laughter binding them together as they faced what was to come, no matter how scary that might be.

From: A.J.
To: Ellie Edwards
Subject: I'm Coming
Hi Ellie,
I've done it. I've booked a flight to Scotland!

From: Ellie Edwards
To: A.J.
Subject: Your Coming
Wow, I am so happy, but I can't talk right now. I must go break my friends out of jail.

From: A.J.
To: Ellie Edwards
Subject:???
What??

CHAPTER 24: **Ellie**

It was nearly midnight as Ellie drove across town. She had never received a call from jail before certainly something to cross off her bucket list, albeit an unwelcome addition. The moon hung low in the sky, casting a silver glow on the empty streets, and with each passing minute, the hum of her thoughts grew louder. Anxiety twisted her stomach into knots as she tried to comprehend the situation. What could have led her friends down such a tumultuous path?

She had driven this route countless times but tonight felt surreal, anxiety clawing at her every second.

Concern gnawed at her insides; what had Amy and Jess done to end up in jail? She envisioned wild scenarios, each more outrageous than the last. Had they gotten into a drunken brawl at a pub, a raucous quarrel over something trivial? Surely that could explain the call. Or worse, was it Jess poisoning Amy in a moment of spite, their relationship crumbling like fragile glass? Ellie shuddered at the vision, imagining heated words exchanged, and the bond they once shared slipping through her fingers. Perhaps Amy had pushed Jess off the picturesque cliffs, in an emotional fit, triggered by another disastrous encounter with Noah, the object of her secret affections.

The possibilities swirled endlessly, each more dreadful than the last. Whatever happened, she hoped they had not hurt each other too badly. No matter how messy friendships became, they were meant to uplift each other. After all, family dramas sometimes ended tragically, and these two had already survived enough friction without jail time added to their list.

With a large shopper bag stuffed to the brim on her shoulder, Ellie hurried into the local police station. Fluorescent lights buzzed overhead, casting an eerie glow on stark white walls and cold metal benches that seemed to swallow any warmth. The air carried a subtle mix of strong coffee and antiseptic, creating an urgency that made her heart pound. She steeled herself for what was to come, determination flaring as she readied herself to rescue her friends. The weight of their friendship fuelled her mission; she refused to leave them stranded, no matter what it took.

Approaching the guard at the front desk, she rehearsed a torrent of words in her mind: an impassioned plea advocating for her friends, or perhaps an elaborate tale highlighting their good hearts.

"I am here to bail out Jess and Amy!" she declared, her voice ringing with conviction, though beneath it lay a current of nervousness.

"I don't care what it takes; I'll pay any fine, hire the best lawyers in town, whatever you need!"

Her determination fuelled her imagination: her friends whisked to safety like in the movies, lots of cash thrown to solve the problem. She knew reality might be far from this bravado, but she allowed herself to dream. Someday, when Shoperapy thrived, her words would carry real weight, and she would genuinely have the means to save her friends.

The guard gave her a bored look, chin resting heavily on his palm, sighing as though time passed far too slowly. Ellie felt irritation rise, but she quickly squashed it. Undeterred, she continued her passionate pitch, detailing imagined injustices and insisting on her friends' good hearts, their need for understanding over punishment.

"You see," she continued, the words tumbling out in a breathless whirl, "they did not mean any harm! They need guidance, not jail!"

Finally, after what felt like an eternity of unreciprocated communication, the guard gestured dismissively with an exaggerated flick of his wrist.

"They're sitting right over there," he muttered.

"They've been free to go for almost half an hour."

The revelation hit her like a tidal wave. Ellie blinked, disbelief giving way to a rush of relief. Half an hour? How could they be sitting there so casually while she had been pacing herself into knots? Determined to get answers, she bolted around the corner, her heart racing.

There they were, Amy and Jess perched comfortably at a police officer's desk, feet propped up as they munched on snacks from a vending machine that had clearly seen better days. The sight made her heart plummet and soar all at once.

"What are you doing?" Ellie exclaimed, incredulity sharp in her voice.

They were deep in animated conversation with the officer, who astonishingly seemed to be enjoying their company, laughing along with them. Plastic cups of coffee sat beside them, evidence they had settled in far longer than she had imagined, indulging in chips and chocolate like it was a late-night hangout rather than a police station.

"Ellie!" they shouted in unison, grinning as though reunited after weeks apart.

"Come join us!"

The cheerfulness was wildly uncoordinated with the panic she had felt earlier, leaving her stunned. She approached slowly, trying to make sense of the bizarre scene.

"What? The guard said you two are free to go?" she asked, still disbelieving as she inspected them for signs of trouble scratches, bruises, anything. But they looked perfectly fine. Relaxed, even. Confusion swirled in her chest.

"What on earth happened back there?"

The officer, leaning casually against the desk, cleared his throat.

"They were caught spray-painting a shop," he said flatly, eyes twinkling with amusement.

The absurdity hit Ellie all at once, and she burst into laughter, the tension finally draining from her shoulders. Everything clicked Jess, her advice, Amy's bottled-up feelings, and an impulsive burst of misplaced creativity. No further explanation was needed.

Ellie crossed her arms, a victorious smirk spreading across her face as a wave of pride washed over her.

"So, my meddling worked out then?" Ellie asked playfully, her eyebrows waggling with delight as she embraced her role as the accidental mastermind of the evening.

"All my secret-sharing about who had a crush on who was for the best, eh?"

The teasing lilt in her voice invited laughter. As she watched Amy and Jess exchange sheepish glances, she knew neither of them wanted to admit she was right. Still, their subtle smiles betrayed them, revealing a bond that had only deepened through the rollercoaster of their lives. Pride swelled in Ellie's chest, and she allowed herself a moment to relish in having saved the day if only by accident. In their own chaotic way, they had all succeeded together.

"Thanks, officer!" Jess chirped, her cheeks still flushed from laughing.

The two women stood, thanking the officer with genuine smiles before making their way towards the exit. Just as freedom beckoned, Ellie felt a sudden pang of disappointment and pouted dramatically, as though caught between worlds.

"Are you sure you don't have to stay here a little longer?" she asked, a touch too eagerly, clinging to the hope that the night's adventure was not quite over.

As a final attempt to keep the moment alive, she hoisted her shopper bag and held it out with flair.

"I brought you something to remember this night by!"

Jess and Amy leaned forward, curiosity lighting up their faces then promptly burst into uncontrollable laughter when they saw what was inside.

Ellie, it turned out, had made a quick detour on her way to the station, scouring nearby shops for the perfect orange jumpsuits to wear inside the *clink*. Bright, unmistakable, and utterly ridiculous, the jumpsuits captured the absurdity of the entire evening perfectly.

As laughter echoed through the station, Ellie watched Jess and Amy revel in the joy of the ridiculousness, warmth radiating from their friendship. It was a surreal moment; one filled with giggles and glee and destined to become an unmissable story they would retell for years to come.

The two women leaned their heads against one another, laughter intertwining and bouncing off the sterile walls of the police station. The sound was infectious, blossoming into a memory that would forever remind them of this night.

"Now," Ellie grinned, "if you want a free ride home with me, you'll need to pull these on quickly. I can't have them going to waste, can I?"

Behind them, the officer shook his head with a chuckle, thoroughly bemused as he watched the trio leave the station clad in bright orange jumpsuits.

He had never seen anything quite so absurd in Meadowbank.

CHAPTER 25 Lily

Lily arrived early at Shoperapy and was surprised to find Ellie already there. Ellie was not exactly known for being an early bird; she had a reputation for rolling in just as the first customer walked through the door. But today was different. As Lily stepped inside, she noticed the soft glow of fairy lights illuminating the shop, casting a warm, inviting ambience. The gentle hum of machinery in the back added a sense of familiarity, wrapping around her as tenderly as the colourful blankets draped over the seating areas.
And what was more, Ellie was not alone.

Jess was there, her vibrant hair a swirling palette of colours bouncing with excitement, and Amy too, wearing a shy yet genuine smile. To Lily's happy surprise, they all seemed to be getting along something she had quietly hoped for but never quite dared to believe would happen. The air was thick with cheerful chatter and shared laughter.

"So," Lily said, tilting her head towards the windows, "I see the vandal struck again, huh?"

Bright splashes of neon green, red, and pink marred the crisp view of the bustling street outside, like unruly bursts of graffiti slapped against the otherwise charming façade of the shop. The colours clashed dramatically with Shoperapy's vibrant tones, adding a surreal edge that immediately piqued Lily's curiosity.

Jess and Amy giggled, their voices light and carefree, cutting through the lingering calm of the morning.

"It's all the rage, apparently. Urban art or whatever," Jess said with a wink, tossing her hair back playfully.

Together, they looked like a trio of mischievous flourishes, weaving silent tales of whatever chaos had unfolded the night before.

"Well, it was *two* vandals this time," Ellie chimed in, a cheeky glint in her eye that Lily found instantly contagious.

"And I suspect much better-dressed vandals at that! Whoever did this clearly have a flair for fashion, though I'm not sure day-glow will catch on along the high street."

Her laughter was infectious.

With uncontainable enthusiasm, Ellie filled Lily in on the night's events, leaning casually against the counter as her hands gestured animatedly.

"They went wild with the spray cans," she explained.

"And we are all eagerly waiting for Noah to come and clean the windows. He should be here any minute, if he remembers the way, that is!"

Sarcasm dripped from her words, but Lily could not help being charmed by her friend's storytelling.

A mouth-watering aroma wafted through the air, causing Lily's stomach to rumble in agreement. The girls had ordered breakfast when hunger struck at five a.m., and the tantalising scents of pancakes, French toast, fresh fruit, and a hearty egg dish filled the shop. There was more food than three girls could possibly eat, the spread laid out like a feast.

No longer dressed in orange jumpsuits, the trio now wore matching cute pyjamas adorned with whimsical animal prints. They had created a cosy little nest by the window pillows and throws arranged into a makeshift lounge, laughter spilling freely between them. An enormous pot of coffee simmered nearby, filling the space with its rich aroma and beckoning Lily to join in.

The atmosphere crackled with youthful, sleep-deprived energy. They had even concocted a cheeky plan to ensure Amy looked amazing when Noah arrived. The excitement in the room was palpable. The idea was to sneak Amy out the back, circle around, and engineer a second *"cute meet"* with the window cleaner an encounter meticulously planned, right down to an intricate hair flip for maximum dramatic effect.

As laughter mingled with the scent of breakfast, Lily settled onto a cushion and munched on pancakes before getting to work opening the shop for the day. The fluffy stacks melted in her mouth, gifting her a brief moment of bliss, untouched by the usual worries of life. She began sorting through her silk-printing supplies, the soothing rhythm of Ellie, Jess, and Amy's chatter drifting over her like a gentle wave. Their animated conversations formed a backdrop of vibrant energy, filling the space with camaraderie that quietly lifted Lily's spirits.

From her spot by the window, she watched the shadows of passers-by drift past, each wrapped in their own stories, their own mornings. Glancing back at her friends, Lily felt a warm rush of happiness as Jess and Amy were finally bonding. It had been hard for Amy; she needed a friend, someone to share her everyday highs and lows with. Shoperapy had become a refuge for her, a haven where she could slowly rebuild her confidence. Lily understood that feeling completely.

This place meant the same to her. It was where she felt she belonged. And yet, doubts stirred at the back of her mind. Thoughts of Dubai tugged at her crowded markets, dancing lights, the constant hum of voices reminding her of the city she had once called home without even thinking about it.

Her thoughts spiralled, contrasting the vibrancy of her past with the softness of her present. Shoperapy, with its laid-back café atmosphere, felt like a sanctuary, yet nostalgia hovered like a lingering shadow. What did it mean to live with memories of one place while planting roots in another? Could she truly embrace this life while her heart still wandered the bustling streets of Dubai? The more she thought about it, the more tangled her emotions became.

Just then, the gentle tinkling of the shop bell announced the arrival of a customer, pulling Lily back from her reflections. She snapped back to reality and turned to meet the curious gaze of a woman whose eyes darted around the room, taking in the scene before her. After casting Ellie, Jess, and Amy a mildly amused look, the woman focused intently on Lily.

"I'm interested in the silk scarves," she said, her voice brimming with intrigue, as though she had uncovered a hidden treasure.

"Of course," Lily replied, pointing towards the back wall. "They're over there with the rest of the accessories."

The silk scarves fluttered softly in the cool breeze of the air conditioning vibrant, textured, lovingly crafted, and draped elegantly like works of art waiting to be admired. The woman smiled, but a glimmer of mischief danced in her eyes as she added,

"No, I meant the silk scarf you're printing on right now."

Lily felt her cheeks flush with embarrassment. She had completely forgotten the scarf laid out on her workstation, the fabric covered in colourful, spontaneous designs she had created without much thought—or any intention of outside judgement.

"Oh sorry," she stammered quickly. "Those are not for sale. I was just… playing around."

The admission felt raw and vulnerable, as though Lily was revealing a cherished secret too soon, one she was not yet ready to share with anyone.

The woman's smile faltered, disappointment flickering briefly across her face.

"Oh… well, they should be," she said lightly.

"And if you ever decide to sell, give me a call."

She handed Lily her business card, then turned on her heel and left without buying anything, her departure swift and faintly regretful.

Lily blinked, stunned, her heart racing just a little too quickly for comfort.

Surely her designs could not be *that* appealing? It was only a hobby a fledgling passion she had barely allowed herself to explore. Self-doubt crept in, gnawing at her insides.

This work was nothing like her gruelling days at the hotel, where she had spent years perfecting her craft, preparing dishes that delighted critics and satisfied demanding patrons. The shift from culinary artistry to textile experimentation felt monumental—and frightening. Yet here, amid soft lighting and gentle laughter, she felt something different. A spark. A quiet sense of joy. The colourful fabric in her hands felt almost magical, transforming uncertainty into expression.

As the door closed behind the customer with a soft thud, Lily felt a pang of doubt tighten in her chest. Why would anyone be interested in her casual experiments with silk? Her gaze drifted back to the scarf laid out before her, its swirling colours dancing under the light. This was not just play, she realised. Perhaps it was something more a budding talent she had not yet dared to acknowledge.

A renewed determination flickered within her. She shook off her doubts and returned to her work, the gentle hum of her friends' chatter wrapping around her like a comforting blanket. Today felt full of possibility. And for the first time in what felt like ages, Lily found herself eager to step into the unknown.

As she wove intricate patterns into the fabric, she felt it a sense of belonging, a quiet hope she thought she had lost somewhere along the way. This was a new beginning. Shoperapy enveloped her like a warm embrace. It was more than a shop; it was a home a place where she could create freely while discovering who she truly was, and who she might become.

Her thoughts were interrupted when her phone buzzed with a call from Teddy. Lily glanced at the screen, then pressed *ignore*. Moments later, a message followed.

T to L: *Please, Lily. We need to talk before you leave. xx*

Lily stared at the screen, wishing her heart felt as light as the woman laughing by the window.

CHAPTER 26: **Amy**

At about midday, just as the girls were animatedly debating what to order for lunch growling stomachs interrupting every other sentence Amy was the first to notice a man approaching down the street. He carried a broom, wore an oversized jacket that flapped in the breeze, and balanced a bucket in one hand and a sturdy ladder in the other. The sun sat high in the sky now, its warmth making the afternoon feel both promising and sluggish. The morning had dragged on, and hunger had returned with force. Thai? Italian? Burgers? The options felt endless, bouncing around the shop like restless thoughts, colliding, and drifting away again.

Ellie's gaze snapped to the window.

"Okay, nobody panics," she announced, excitement and urgency lacing her voice. "It is go time."

The girls exchanged looks, sparks of anticipation igniting instantly. The phrase became their rallying cry, and the air buzzed with expectation. They sprang into action, chatter and giggles filling the shop with purpose. Jess grabbed her phone to scan local menus, her fingers flying across the screen, while Amy bolted towards the bathroom, determined to freshen up before fate arrived.

She splashed cool water over her face, the shock grounding her racing thoughts. A quick spritz of her favourite perfume soft, floral, comforting lingered like a whispered promise. She slipped into the dress they had all agreed on: chic, effortless, the perfect balance of casual and special. Something that said *I look good for myself*, not *I planned this all night*. The fabric skimmed her body beautifully, twirling slightly as she moved. Catching her reflection in the mirror, her heart thudded harder. The thought of seeing Noah again sent butterflies scattering wildly through her chest.

But as she reached behind her to zip the dress, a sound drifted in from the front of the shop.

"Oh."

Jess's voice short, sharp, wrong.

The single word sent a jolt of unease through Amy's veins.

What does that mean? Panic flared instantly. That was not part of the plan.

The thrill of anticipation twisted into a tight knot of dread, freezing her in place. The fabric pooled around her legs like a cocoon, suddenly heavy with unravelling thoughts. The air felt thick and charged.

Then Ellie's voice floated through the shop.

"Hi, you must be here to clean the windows."

Amy's heart sank.

Why would Ellie say that… if it was Noah?

The excitement they had carefully built fractured, replaced by a creeping, hollow discomfort. The world outside dulled into a distant hum as doubt flooded in. Something was not right.

Her fingers trembled against the cool metal of the zipper as she slowly peeked out of the dressing room. Jess was approaching her now, sympathy and disappointment written plainly across her face.

Panic surged.

The shop blurred, the walls closing in as Amy stood frozen in that small space, her temporary refuge, feeling it buckle under the weight of everything she had not been prepared to lose.

"It's not him, is it?" she asked, each word heavy with grief. Doubt clawed at her insides as a bittersweet sorrow settled deep in her stomach. The silence that followed felt suffocating, as though the world itself had paused, waiting for the answer to land.

Jess shook her head slowly, her expression soft with empathy.

"I'm so sorry, Amy."

The words struck like a dull ache, draining the joy from the air. She had wanted *needed* this to be a fairy-tale moment, where they would collide unexpectedly and everything would fall into place, like stars aligning in a perfectly timed sky.

A smile flickered across Amy's face, but it was fragile, a flimsy mask stretched over spiralling disappointment.

"It is nothing. Do not worry about it. It was silly anyway," she said, though the quiver in her voice betrayed the lie.

Each heartbeat echoed loudly in her ears, amplifying the ache that wrapped around her like a tightening shroud.

Back inside the sanctuary of the dressing room, Amy fought the tears threatening to spill. She had honestly believed today would be different that whatever spark they had shared before would reignite with just one look. Without meaning to, she had nurtured daydreams: their first date, laughter folded into quiet conversations, the warmth of shared coffee, the thrill of almost-too-reckless moments. Would he lean in to kiss her? Would she let him?

Now, those dreams dissolved, evaporating into thin air, leaving only their hollow echoes behind.

Disappointment pooled bitterly in her stomach, followed by a surge of self-directed anger. She was furious with herself for hoping at all. Hope, she realised, had been the spark that ignited her foolish fantasies. Maybe she lived too often in a fairy-tale version of reality. Maybe she deserved this sting proof that not every wish was meant to come true. The reflection staring back at her showed more than a ruined outfit; it revealed the wall she had carefully built to protect herself.

With a sharp exhale, Amy changed quickly back into her pyjamas, no longer interested in hiding behind a forced smile. Instead, she formed a new resolve one where she would not rely on romantic possibilities for meaning or reassurance. Squaring her shoulders, she took a steadying breath and stepped out of the dressing room, ready to face whatever came next.

Ellie and Jess were waiting, already rallying behind her, enthusiasm spilling over as they suggested fun outfits and bold shoes, determined to lift her spirits.

"It's not the end of the world," Ellie said firmly, her voice infused with warmth and stubborn optimism.

"We will find him. We will create an even better run-in than the one we planned. Do not give up."

Ellie's resilience injected a faint spark of life back into the heavy atmosphere, lifting Amy's spirits, even if only slightly.

But Amy waved it away, forcing a shrug.

"I am fine, you know. It is nothing."

The words wavered under the weight of their concerned stares, and for a fleeting moment, uncertainty washed over her like fog, blurring the line between what she wanted to believe and what she already knew.

"Come on, at least let us grab lunch or a coffee… something!" Jess implored, an insistent sparkle in her eyes, quiet determination radiating from her as she nudged Amy gently. Their bond felt unbreakable, grounding.

"Really, I'm okay," Amy insisted, though a flicker of doubt crept into her voice, betraying the calm she tried to project. Inside, an uneasy contradiction churned the warmth of her friends pressed up against the disappointment still clawing at her heart.

As they prepared to leave, Jess's laughter blended with Ellie's earnest reassurances, creating a cocoon of friendship around Amy. Yet the contrast was sharp: the joy surrounding her glimmered brightly while her disappointment lingered in the shadows. She inhaled deeply, taking in the scent of jasmine mixed with coffee and fabric, and with it, a bittersweet awareness of what might have been.

Outside, the world continued turning. New beginnings seemed to hover at every street corner, and Amy realised she had not faced this moment alone. Whatever happiness she was building, it was supported steadied by Ellie and Jess.

In the end, she decided, the day was not a failure. It was simply another step on her messy, beautiful path—one where laughter could still rise above tears, and friendship could bloom even in the quiet ache of longing. The thought softened her expression. Life was unpredictable, after all, and sometimes the warmth of shared moments mattered more than any fragile daydream of love.

As they stepped outside, sunlight kissed their faces, and a small flicker of hope stirred within Amy. She was surrounded by people who cared. For today, that was enough. There would be other days, other chances just not, perhaps, with Noah.

She told them she was tired, behind on work, and needed to scrub the spray paint from her fingers.

Amy thanked Ellie and Jess sincerely, but still chose to leave, declining their offers to stay longer.

She had learned something important: whatever she felt for Noah was not meant for her, and for now, that truth was enough.

Blog
Posted: 11:22 pm (GMT)
User: Your Fashion Ellie-vator
Subscribers: 378

Hey everyone,

It's Ellie here. I just wanted to share something deeply personal with you all. A few weeks ago, I felt ashamed and not the best of friend to anyone. I will not lie; it felt as though the community I had created at Shoperapy had crumbled. I found myself lost in a mix of emotions, grappling with sadness and confusion.

In my previous posts, I glossed over what I was feeling, not wanting to burden you with my troubles. But, reading your overwhelmingly caring messages made me realise just how mistaken I was. Honesty is key, not just in life, but in sharing my experiences with you.

Your kindness prompted me to reflect on the importance of vulnerability in our connections. So many of you shared your own stories of heartache, and that bond helped me realise this journey, we call life, isn't just about me; it is about all of us woman supporting one another.

So, thank you for your empathy! I promise to be more open in my blog from now on. I can't wait to continue sharing my stories about fashion, heartbreaks, and the goings on in Meadowbank.

Much love, Ellie xx

CHAPTER 27: **Sara**

Since the 'Secrets Night' at Shoperapy, Sara had tried more times than she could count to summon the courage to tell her mum about her relationship with Charlie. Each moment felt pivotal, the right opportunity hovering just within reach, yet somehow, she always faltered. Anxiety churned in her stomach like a heavy stone, weighing her down. She rehearsed endlessly, scripting the perfect confession in her mind thrilling, terrifying, so close to spilling out— only for it to slip away before she could make it real.

In the grocery store aisle, surrounded by brightly coloured protein bars, her heart raced as she stared at the neatly stacked boxes. Each one seemed to taunt her, daring her to tell the truth. She picked up a neon-blue protein bar, its glossy wrapper glittering beneath the fluorescent lights, and asked casually,

"Do you think we should try this one, Mum?"

It was a cover, nothing more. What she really wanted was to scream,

I'm dating Charlie!

But the words vanished, like grains of sand slipping through her fingers.

Other shoppers bustled past, oblivious to the turmoil unfolding inside her, and Sara wondered how she would ever find the strength to say it out loud.

At the gym, during a gentle pre-birth workout session with her cousin Cameron, she made a quiet promise to herself. The clang of weights and the steady hum of movement filled the space, yet she felt alone in her thoughts.

After this set, she told herself, focusing on the lift, *I will tell her.*

But the moment came and went when Cameron bounded over, cheerfully announcing they could push through five more minutes on the stepper. Her resolve crumbled under the weight of his enthusiasm, her courage dissolving into the rhythm of routine.

"Five? Cameron, you really are a hard taskmaster," she laughed. "I thought we were finished!"

Later, at her mum's favourite little spot by the beach, Sara sat across from Victoria, the soothing sound of waves lapping against the shore filling the air. Salt mingled with the comforting scent of fried fish and chips, grounding her while simultaneously amplifying her anxiety. She rehearsed her speech again as the server approached.

I will do it before the mints, she promised herself, hoping the familiar flavours would steady her nerves.

But, like the tide, the moment slipped away. Laughter replaced nerves as she and Victoria shared dessert another cherished tradition and once again, the truth lodged itself firmly in her throat.

There was always something. Another shopper asking Victoria about protein bar brands. Cameron rambling on about his next fitness regime. In the restaurant, a nearby table erupted into a boisterous birthday song, filling the room with joyous noise while Sara sat frozen. Her fork and knife trembling in her hands.

She felt trapped by timing, by expectation, by herself.

The small joys of life had become bittersweet, tinged with the quiet anxiety of carrying a secret she could not yet release.

In truth, it was fear that held her back. Fear of her mum's reaction. Fear of the disappointment that might flicker across Victoria's face. Fear of the conversations that would change everything.

They were a strong unit, her, and her mum, capable of facing almost anything together. Almost!

Later that evening, they sat together on the couch, a bowl of low-fat popcorn balanced precariously between them its virtue thoroughly ruined by the handfuls of M&Ms they had tossed in for good measure. Each sweet, crunchy bite offered a small comfort, a welcome distraction. Victoria chatted absently about the latest reality show she was hooked on, her voice drifting into a soft, familiar hum.

Sara barely heard her.

Her thoughts churned relentlessly, her heart pounding as she fixated on the secret lodged deep in her chest. Would it make things better if she told her mum? Or would it fracture the easy closeness they shared? Would this confession rewrite everything?

Without warning before doubt could reclaim control… she blurted out,

"I'm dating Charlie!"

The words escaped as if they had a will of their own. No preparation. No rehearsing. Just do it. Wasn't that the slogan of her mum's favourite sports brand, after all?

The silence that followed felt electric.

Sara's heart raced, excitement and dread tangling tightly in her chest. To her horror, she seemed almost as shocked by her own confession as her mum was. Victoria froze mid-bite, a piece of popcorn hovering halfway to her mouth. Confusion washed over her face, the wheels clearly turning as she tried to make sense of what she had just heard.

"Who's Charlie?" Victoria asked, her forced casualness unconvincing.

Heat crept up Sara's cheeks. She bit her lip, hesitation clawing its way back in.

"You know who Charlie is…" she murmured, attempting a lightness she did not feel.

Victoria laughed, but there was no warmth in it. Her eyes widened, disbelief hardening into concern.

"No. No, you don't mean *our* Charlie," she said quickly. "Because *our* Charlie is your father's best friend. *Our* Charlie gave you lollipops when you were a child. *Our* Charlie is nearly thirty years older than you!"

"Mum, I know that you and Dad already know," Sara replied earnestly, her fingers tightening instinctively around the bowl between them.

Victoria exhaled slowly, the sigh heavy, weighted with too many thoughts left unsaid. Silence settled over the room, thick and suffocating. The television murmured on in the background, but its noise faded into irrelevance as Victoria's gaze fixed on Sara searching, questioning.

"I don't understand how this even happened," Victoria said at last; her voice strained with disbelief and unanswered questions.

Sara felt emotion swell again, threatening to spill over. She inhaled deeply, grounding herself, determined not to retreat now.

"I came home one day after I found out I was pregnant," she began, her voice steady despite the storm raging inside her. The words felt enormous, irreversible, yet once started, they rushed out.

"I was distraught, Mum. I didn't know what to do and Charlie happened to come in while he was looking for Dad."

"He was so kind, so mature," Sara continued, the memory of Charlie's reassuring smile carving a warm space in her heart.

"He listened to me, offered advice without judging. I have never had a man treat me that way, and it felt... refreshing." A flicker of vulnerability crossed her face.

"I've been so used to immature jerks at university..."

Victoria sighed, her expression shifting between concern and contemplation as she absorbed her daughter's words. The pause hung heavy in the air, thick with unspoken fears.

"No, honey... this isn't good for you," her mother said finally, her tone gentle but firm.

"He's too old. He is not right for you."

Sara's emotions surged. Her heart raced, defiance rising alongside urgency.

"But Mum!" she protested. "Charlie is just as excited about this baby as I am, even though it's not his!"

A flicker of memory crossed Victoria's eyes, a faint gasp escaping her lips as she recalled Charlie's own losses.

"You know Charlie and his wife wanted a child desperately before she tragically passed away from cancer after their marriage, right?" Sara's voice trembled slightly yet remained steady.

"It's been hard for him too."

A flicker of memory crossed Victoria's eyes, a faint gasp escaping her lips as she recalled Charlie's own losses.

The words felt like a bridge, connecting her heart to her mother's understanding.

Victoria nodded slowly, brow furrowed in thought. The tension ebbed slightly as she looked at Sara not just as a daughter, but as a young woman navigating life's complex choices. Though she struggled with the age difference, a flicker of hope sparked in her gaze.

"Maybe…" Victoria began cautiously. "Maybe it could be a nice new chance for Charlie. But still, I worry."

Her words lingered in the air, threaded with care, concern, and the tentative willingness to consider something unexpected.

As their conversation continued, Sara felt a weight lift from her shoulders, a release of tension she had not realized she'd been holding. The room seemed lighter, more open. For the first time, speaking her truth felt less terrifying. She shared her excitement, her hopes, and the bond she had forged with Charlie. Her words poured warmth into the space that had once felt shadowed and uncertain.

By the evening's close, Sara sensed a newfound clarity. Perhaps the love she shared with Charlie could become something beautiful and lasting. And in the gentle exchange, she felt her mum, still wary, beginning to recognize the promise in Sara's choice.

Sara knew her mum wasn't fully on board yet. But the hardest part was done. She had come clean. No more secrets. And, as Ellie had reminded her, somehow, it would all work out. Maybe not in the way she expected… but somehow.

CHAPTER 28: Ellie

It was finally the day Ellie had been waiting for, her mystery man from Dubai was arriving soon, and excitement coursed through her veins. As she finished getting ready in her small, sunlit flat, she imagined Amir flying high over France, crossing oceans and distances just to reach her. It felt a little crazy to be so thrilled over someone she had never met, and yet the anticipation was undeniably intoxicating. She practically danced around the room, telling Chase, her friend who had come to help her get ready, how over the moon she felt.

"Good luck!" Chase said with his usual cheeky grin, heading towards the door. His enthusiasm was contagious, and Ellie felt a warm surge of gratitude.

"Thanks! I appreciate it!" she called after him, taking one last glance in the mirror to make sure every auburn strand fell perfectly and that her outfit reflected the vibrant persona she wanted to show the world. Butterflies fluttered frantically in her stomach, gearing her up for the meeting ahead, while her imagination spun through a hundred romantic possibilities.

Ellie hurried to Shoperapy, her beloved boutique and sanctuary for fashion lovers, each corner infused with her personality. As she stepped inside, she inhaled deeply the comforting scent of fresh fabrics mingled with the enticing aroma of coffee from the back room. Today was special; she was unveiling exclusive new dresses from Dubai, and everything had to be perfect. Each dress seemed to hold a personality of its own, vibrant patterns yearning for a wearer who would appreciate them. The thought sent a rush of excitement through Ellie as she pictured eager customers clutching her creations.

Grace appeared, bustling with her trademark energy, arranging displays, and crafting an inviting atmosphere designed to captivate every passerby.

"Did you see the new dresses?" Ellie exclaimed, her eyes sparkling as she held up a dazzling maxi dress that shimmered under the soft shop lights. The copper tones caught the rays beautifully, almost like a star twinkling on a summer night.

"This one will be a huge hit!" Ellie added, imagining the joy it would bring to some lucky customer, how it might flatter their figure, inspire confidence, and even lead to a successful date.

Grace grinned, a playful gleam in her eyes.

"You could wear it on your second date!" she teased, nudging Ellie gently.

The thought of a second date with Amir made Ellie blush a delightful mix of embarrassment and excitement. Yet a part of her remained grounded; while the idea of romance thrilled her, her responsibility to the shop and her customers came first. Every interaction mattered, and she poured her heart into her work.

Later, glancing at the clock, she realized the moment was approaching. The shop bell rang, slicing through the soft hum of the boutique, and Ellie's heart skipped. A man entered tall, dark-haired, with tousled waves and eyes that sparkled with intrigue. His confident smile sent butterflies fluttering in her stomach, and Ellie felt a rush of nervous exhilaration. Perhaps her heart's desires were finally stepping out of imagination and into reality.

"Shopping for someone special?"

Ellie asked, forcing her voice to stay steady and professional, despite the flutter racing through her chest. There was something undeniably magnetic about him an ease, a presence that made the air feel charged. She found herself hoping, irrationally, that whoever he was shopping for truly deserved whatever she helped him choose.

"I am indeed," he replied, his voice warm and smooth, lingering just long enough to make her pulse jump.

"I want to get her something really special she can wear on a date."

Ellie smiled, curiosity blooming as she gestured around the shop.

"Well, you've come to the right place. This shop is full of special things. What does she like?"

She leaned in slightly, eager now, every second heightening her anticipation as she tried unsuccessfully to ignore the spark buzzing between them.

He studied her for a moment, fingers brushing his chin, a playful glint in his eyes.

"What do *you* like?" he asked. "She looks a lot like you."

Ellie's heart skipped. The compliment landed softly but decisively, sending warmth rushing through her. She laughed, genuine and bright.

"Well, I love bold colours," she said, her enthusiasm spilling through before she could stop it.

Reaching for a dress alive with vibrant patterns, she held it up proudly, the fabric catching the light.

"This one's perfect and it's all the way from Dubai."

Their playful rhythm flowed effortlessly, laughter weaving between them as something unspoken took shape. Chemistry like this was rare, and Ellie felt it clear, undeniable.

He chuckled, nodding approvingly.

"I think you're absolutely right. That's an excellent choice."

When he agreed to buy it, Ellie's smile widened instinctively. But just before he left, he paused, handing the dress back to her. His eyes sparkled with quiet certainty as he spoke.

"Perhaps you'll wear it tonight," he said gently. "On our dinner date."

Ellie froze, surprise flashing across her face followed by a rush of exhilarating clarity.

Amir was standing right in front of her.

CHAPTER 29: Lily

Lily walked into Shoperapy, hitting *ignore* once again on a call from Teddy. The messages he'd left over the past few nights had robbed her of sleep, looping endlessly in her mind. What was she supposed to do? The stress of her personal life clung to her like a weight, but the shop with its bright displays and cheerful ambience had become her sanctuary. The soothing scents of vanilla, jasmine, and freshly cut flowers offered at least a moment's peace amid the chaos of her thoughts.

Yet as she stepped inside, her heartbeat quickened, anticipation tangled tightly with anxiety. Could today finally be the day she escaped her worries, if only briefly? She needed a distraction something to pull her away from Teddy and their unresolved mess and the lively hum of Shoperapy felt like exactly the tonic she needed.

As she eased through the doorway, the familiar sights and sounds began to work their magic. The ambient chatter of customers browsing the aisles, Grace's cheerful laughter, and the gentle clinking of coffee cups blended into a comforting symphony that wrapped around Lily like a warm embrace.

Then she froze.

Right in the centre of Shoperapy where customers usually lingered, laughing and browsing, a man dropped down onto one knee. His posture was confident, his expression animated as he prepared to propose to Ellie. Grace stood beside them, one hand clamped over her mouth, vibrating with excitement and disbelief.

The scene felt surreal, almost absurd. Lily blinked, her mind scrambling to catch up with what her eyes were seeing.

Then recognition hit her like a thunderclap.

"Amir!" she exclaimed, her heart pounding violently in her chest.

Her brother.

The same Amir who had always been fearless, flamboyant, and wildly romantic turned his head, glancing over his shoulder with a sheepish grin completely at ease, as though proposing in the middle of a boutique was the most natural thing in the world.

Did he even consider how utterly mad this looked? Her mind raced with a barrage of questions as she fought past the mounting tide of confusion. After all, Amir had always been the more adventurous sibling, throwing caution to the wind in his quest for love. But this bold proclamation took things to an entirely new level, and Lily's stomach churned at the thought of it. What if this impulsive moment spiralled beyond their control?

"Oh, hi, sister!" he said casually, giving her a small wave.

Lily's stomach dropped.

What on earth was he doing proposing to Ellie? In public. In her shop. Without warning. Did he realise how utterly mad this looked? Questions collided in her mind as panic surged through her veins. Amir had always chased love with reckless enthusiasm, but this was something else entirely.

The contrast between them couldn't have been sharper. Her heart thundered with alarm while he radiated effortless confidence, that infuriating grin firmly in place as he turned his attention back to Ellie either oblivious to Lily's turmoil or completely unconcerned by it.

A swell of dread washed over her. What if this went wrong? What if this impulsive moment spiralled beyond control? The stakes felt enormous, the situation fragile, and Lily could almost feel the consequences hovering in the air.

She stood rooted to the spot, far too stunned to process his nonchalance, her thoughts racing as the moment unfolded before her.

"Ellie, that's my brother!" Lily stammered, disbelief etched across her face as she pointed almost accusingly in Amir's direction.

Panic washed over her as the full enormity of the situation struck like a romantic comedy plot twist that had spiralled wildly out of control. Why would Amir, her adventurous yet notoriously reckless brother, leap into something this monumental after a single encounter? The thought sent her emotions into freefall. In the world of love, this was an all-out bungee jump with no safety cord attached.

Her mind collided with a thousand thoughts at once: concern for Amir's well-being, frustration at his impulsiveness, and confusion over how she herself was supposed to react. She feared what might happen next how spectacularly this could implode if it went wrong.

Amir waved a dismissive hand back at her, as though her concerns were mere trivialities in the grand scheme of love.

"Lily, if you don't mind," he called out, his focus glued to Ellie, whose astonished expression mirrored Lily's disbelief.

Both women watched him expectantly as the air thickened with suspense. Amir took a breath and launched into the heartfelt speech he had clearly rehearsed. Lily, however, felt her legs give way beneath her. She crumpled onto the plush couch in the corner.

What was he thinking?

Surely, he understood the weight of what he was doing. Just nights ago, they'd joked over drinks about the absurdity of love, how ridiculous people became when emotions clouded logic. And now this? A dramatic public proposal after a handful of emails and one fateful meeting in Dubai? It felt like jumping headfirst out a plane without a parachute.

As much as Lily admired Amir's fearless nature, dread coiled tightly in her chest. Was this courage or recklessness disguised as romance?

The room held its breath as Amir pressed on, clearly determined to mesmerise Ellie with what was shaping up to be a very elaborate monologue. Lily watched, equal parts captivated and horrified, as her brother's theatrics unfolded in agonising slow motion. She was caught between admiration for his boldness and fear that his entire future hinged on this one extravagant moment.

Around them, customers began to gather. Heads peeked out from between clothing racks; baristas paused mid-task, curiosity written plainly across their faces. Lily's heart sank. If this went wrong, it wouldn't be quiet it would be spectacular.

"It's been a whirlwind, I know," he began, his voice rising and falling like an orchestra building towards a crescendo.

"We haven't known each other for long, and most of our communication has been through emails. But I believe in the power of connection because when you know, you know. Trust me… I know."

His sincerity was disarming, the kind that could melt even the iciest sceptic. The surrounding customers leaned in, as though drawn by an invisible force.

"The moment we collided in Dubai, I felt something shift," he continued.

"The second I saw your passport lying on the ground, I knew it had to be fate and I thought to myself, *now there's a woman worth pursuing.*"

Amir's words painted romantic imagery in Lily's mind that was almost comical. Her brother had quite literally tripped over the object of his affections and look where it had led him. A delightful mix of horror and amusement bubbled inside her as he continued, spinning enchantment from chaos, crafting the moment into something both compelling and utterly absurd. There was no denying it: Amir had charm. His unabashed enthusiasm was spellbinding, his ability to weave a narrative theatrical yet strangely sincere, as though this were a performance destined to be remembered.

Around her, whispers rippled through the shop, punctuated by sharp intakes of breath from customers drawn into the spectacle strangers witnessing romance unfold in real time, unable to look away.

"I can't picture my life without you, Ellie," Amir said earnestly, his eyes shining brighter than the shop's lights.

"I want to spend the rest of it making you happy. And I would never ask you to give up your precious shop on the contrary, I want to see it thrive. We'll take it to Dubai, where the fashion scene is booming!"

His enthusiasm flooded the room, and despite herself, Lily felt her initial fear loosen its grip. It was as if the universe had leaned in to remind her of life's beautiful unpredictability. Still, beneath the sparkle lingered uncertainty. She felt suspended inside a fantasy one shimmering with excitement and dread in equal measure. Could someone truly be this fearless? This certain?

Amir pressed on, painting a vivid picture of a shared future.

"Just imagine it, Ellie. Shoperapy flourishing under the golden sun of Dubai. I believe in you. You have everything it takes to create something extraordinary. Your emails, your honesty, your passion for life, they lit a fire in me. You are the woman who would step into the unknown with me. The woman I've been searching for."

His words wrapped the room in emotion, transforming curiosity into quiet awe. Lily's heart thudded in time with the weight of his confession. Against her better judgement, she found herself rooting for him even as unease curled in her stomach. What if this ended badly? What if it didn't?

As Amir poured his heart into the space between them, tension thickened the air. Lily braced herself for rejection. Surely Ellie would laugh this off, gently but firmly remind him of reality.

But she didn't.

Ellie stood still, cheeks flushed, her smile soft and radiant like stars appearing at dusk.

"Amir," she said, her voice trembling with emotion, "I'm incredibly flattered. The life you've imagined for us sounds amazing… but I'll need time to think."

Relief crashed over Amir like a breaking wave. His face lit up with unfiltered joy as he stepped forward and pressed a gentle kiss to Ellie's cheek tender, hopeful, reverent. The audience erupted into hushed excitement, whispers fluttering through the shop like released breath.

Lily remained seated on the couch, jaw slack, heart racing, stunned by the unexpected turn her day and perhaps all of their lives had just taken.

With all eyes fixed on Amir and Ellie, a strange intoxication settled over Lily, leaving her quietly reeling from her brother's audacity. She let out a soft, nervous chuckle, suspended between gratitude and disbelief at how wildly unpredictable life could be. Who would have imagined that Amir's theatrical flair would culminate in something so unexpectedly monumental?

The vibrant atmosphere of Shoperapy pulsed with the energy of a love story on the brink of unfolding, the promise of adventure crackling through the air like static electricity. As Lily attempted to steady her thoughts, Grace shot her an incredulous look, sparking a silent, comical exchange of disbelief between them. They had shared countless moments within these walls, but this one stood

"Do you think she'd really move her shop to Dubai for someone she's only spoke to online until now?"

Grace whispered, eyes wide with curiosity and mischief as they watched Amir enthusiastically regain his composure, clearly ready to charm Ellie all over again.

"Let's just hope he has a plan," Lily replied, a knot of emotion tightening in her chest.

Memories of childhood conversations flooded back late-night dreams, bold declarations, promises of futures filled with laughter and adventure. Back then, everything had seemed possible. But this? This felt like stepping clean off the edge of the map, a leap into uncharted territory.

As Amir launched back into his animated declarations, the spectacle resumed equal parts theatrical performance and romantic chaos. The crowd hovered between enchantment and disbelief, unsure whether they were witnessing a love story or a beautifully absurd leap of faith. Lily found herself smiling despite everything. There was something admirable about Amir's audacity. Maybe just maybe it wasn't foolish at all.

Her heart still raced as the realisation settled in: love demanded boldness. It required stepping into the unknown with nothing but hope and courage as armour. In the middle of everyday chaos, love had a way of transforming the ordinary into something extraordinary a reminder that sometimes the heart moved faster than the mind could keep up.

Lily was amazed.

Perhaps what she had always labelled as ridiculous wasn't ridiculous at all. Maybe she had simply been afraid.

And thinking of Teddy of the calls she kept ignoring, the words left unsaid Lily felt something shift inside her. A quiet resolve took shape.

Maybe it was time to leap. Time to be a little reckless. Time to be brave like her brother. Time to stop being afraid.

**You are cordially invited to a
Dubai Party Night @ Shoperapy**

Look out your glam gowns and come join us, and taste the delights of Dubai from Shawarma, and Falafel to desserts such as Luqaimat.
Not only will you taste Dubai delights, but you will get the chance to try on some Dubai inspired fashion.
You don't want to miss this!
See you gorgeous peeps!
**Friday @7:30pm
Love Ellie Xx**

CHAPTER 30: Amy

Amy was just as surprised as anyone that she had agreed to attend Shoperapy's next event when Jess asked - A Dubai Night.

After failing to find Noah again, she had been rigidly certain that life would simply snap back into place back to nights spent alone, endless work hours, and the familiar ache of loneliness that had taken up permanent residence in her chest. Her apartment had grown too quiet, the silence echoing with memories of better days she tried not to revisit.

But her soon-to-be sister-in-law, Jess, turned out to be far more stubborn than Amy had anticipated a quality she secretly admired.

"Come on, Amy! You cannot sit at home all night wallowing in self-pity," Jess had insisted, eyes sparkling as they clinked cocktail glasses at a rooftop bar.

"It's time you got out there and actually *lived* again."

Jess had been relentless, a cheerleader with unwavering faith that Amy still had a spark worth rescuing. And annoyingly it worked. It took more than a couple of Cosmopolitans and a generous dose of laughter to coax out something resembling the old Amy, but eventually, there she was: locking her door and stepping into another Friday night.

As she crossed town towards a party that promised to be loud, crowded, and dare she admit it fun, a strange blend of excitement and dread coursed through her. What if she didn't belong anymore? What if she had lost the version of herself who once thrived in moments like this?

Jess's voice echoed in her head, urging her forward.

When Amy reached the block where Shoperapy sat glowing against the night, laughter and music spilled into the street. Yet something felt off. A subtle tension prickled at the base of her neck.

Then she saw it.

As she rounded the corner, her steps slowed. Someone stood close to the wall ahead, arm moving in sharp, deliberate strokes. At first, her mind refused to register what she was seeing, but recognition hit a second later.

Spray paint.

Her stomach tightened as curiosity tangled with caution. She moved closer, heart pounding, and the truth snapped into focus.

She had caught him red-handed.

Adrenaline surged through her veins, electricity sparking beneath her skin. A quick glance around confirmed her unease the side street was eerily quiet. Restaurant windows glowed warmly nearby, diners absorbed in conversations that felt miles away. No police. No witnesses. Just the soft hiss of spray paint and her own racing pulse.

It was unsettlingly calm. Too calm. Especially when she remembered how differently things had ended the last time she and Jess had flirted with rebellion, spray cans in hand, laughter bubbling over, only narrowly escaping the law.

This time felt different. And Amy knew, with sudden clarity, that whatever she had stumbled into tonight was about to change the course of her evening and possibly far more than that.

Never one for taking risks or for bravery, Amy battled every instinct telling her to walk away. Yet, her feet stayed rooted to the pavement. Something deeper held her there.

Before she could change her mind, she drew in a breath and stepped forward.

"Stop what you're doing and turn around. Now."

She barely recognised her own voice firm, commanding—though doubt curled beneath it like smoke.

To her astonishment, the vandal froze mid-spray. The can hissed once more before falling silent. Slowly, he raised both hands in surrender, but he didn't turn.

Dressed head to toe in black, his hood pulled low, he felt less like a person and more like a threat waiting to reveal itself. Panic flared. What if she had misjudged this entirely? Her heart thundered in her chest, reminding her she wasn't built for confrontations like this.

Who was this woman she'd become standing alone in a dark side street, cloaked in courage she didn't remember possessing? The truth was that the threat was a bluff. Amy had no plan. No backup. Just adrenaline and impulse driving her forward.

Seconds stretched painfully.

Then, at last, the vandal turned.

Amy's breath caught.

"Are you going to apprehend me?" he asked lightly, a crooked smirk tugging at his mouth.

She stared into his eyes and the world tilted.

"Noah!"

Warmth rushed through her, swift and disorienting, her pulse fluttering wildly. The man she had searched for, wondered about, tried and failed to forget standing here, spray paint in hand, as if the universe had orchestrated the most absurd reunion imaginable.

He wasn't a delinquent.

He was *him*.

The rush of emotion felt dangerously familiar, stirring something she thought had long since been buried—the giddy, reckless excitement of falling in love before heartbreak taught her caution.

"But… you're the window cleaner," she managed, the words tumbling out as her mind scrambled to make sense of the moment.

Noah's grin deepened, equal parts mischievous and magnetic.

"I am many things," he said, his voice low and playful, a spark of challenge gleaming in his eyes.

And just like that, Amy knew this night, this choice, this man was about to unravel everything she thought she had accepted.

"I'm also a charming rogue."

Amy's world tilted on its axis. How could this be happening? Had he been right there all along, hidden in plain sight, while she'd been drowning in thoughts of him? Had he seen her through the windows of Shoperapy, moving through her days, quietly yearning for a glimpse of him without ever knowing he was watching too?

Noah observed her turmoil with unmistakable amusement.

"So," he said lightly, one eyebrow arching. "What's it going to be?"

Was he really asking if she would turn him in? Could she even consider it when he stirred feelings she had sworn were long buried? Feelings she had carefully locked away to protect herself.

Amy bit her lip, her emotions swirling like a tempest. Should she feel anger? Should she feel relief? All she could think about was the magnetic pull he had over her, how easily he made her forget the careful plan she had made to shut herself off from the world. Even though it felt surreal, she was suddenly conscious of her emotions again… vibrant, alive, and intoxicatingly real.

Then, without thinking, she reached down and retrieved a can of paint that had rolled away during the commotion.

Noah's bright eyes followed her movements with keen interest, an eager smile still fixed on his lips, the embodiment of mischief.

"Maybe you can show me a thing or two. My first try was rather pitiful, if I'm being honest…" she suggested, hardly believing the words tumbling from her mouth.

The spontaneity startled her, yet it ignited something within her, a thrill of adventure.

As Noah stepped closer, their gazes locked in a moment of understanding that shimmered in the charged atmosphere between them. Amy felt the thrill of the unknown wash over her, invigorating her spirit. Instead of an arrest, she found herself standing on the precipice of something utterly unforeseen, a chance to rediscover a part of herself that had been hidden away, an opportunity to step outside her carefully constructed bubble and embrace spontaneity.

The warmth of the evening enveloped them as chatter and laughter from the party faded into the background, creating a cocoon just for them. Amy considered this newly opened adventure, and her heart raced with excitement.

"Show me then," she challenged playfully, laughter bubbling at her lips. "But if I get caught, you're taking the fall!"

As the first splatters of paint hit the wall, both Amy and Noah couldn't hide their excitement.

Amy bit her lip, thinking hard. Then she reached down and picked up a can of paint. Noah watched her intensely, his eyes bright, a smile still on his lips.

Noah's laugh was deep and infectious, sending a shiver straight through her. Something shifted not loudly, not dramatically, but undeniably. A promise lingered in the air, unspoken yet powerful.

Amy had no idea where this night would lead. But with every stroke of paint and every shared laugh, she felt herself rediscovering the thrill of being alive. The page had turned and whatever came next would take her anywhere but back to solitude.

CHAPTER 31: Sara

Sara's hand was slick with sweat in Charlie's grip as they stood outside Shoperapy, the vibrant buzz of the party spilling through the double doors and teasing her senses. Excitement lingered just beyond the threshold, but beneath it churned a tide of anxiety she couldn't ignore. She had already tried to turn back a dozen times, each imagined retreat heavier than the last. *Is this really a good idea?*

Her mind replayed every moment that had led her here the rehearsed excuses, the reassurances she'd whispered to herself all of which had slowly dissolved into a gnawing sense of dread. With each passing second, her nerves tightened, her stomach fluttering violently as uncertainty clawed at her chest. Breathing felt like work.

Charlie, by contrast, seemed untouched by her inner storm. Steady and assured, he radiated a quiet calm that grounded her, if only slightly. As they reached the entrance, he lifted her hand and pressed a gentle kiss to her palm. Warmth bloomed across her cheeks as he met her gaze, his confidence unwavering.

"It's all going to be alright," he said softly. "I promise."

Then, with a faint smile, "It might even be fun."

Sara wished her heart believed him. Instead, doubt pressed harder as real as the moisture clinging to her skin. Her parents' disapproval echoed in her thoughts: her father's tight-lipped silence, her mother's carefully measured concern. Each interaction replayed like a warning.

What will they say? Can they ever accept this?

The questions circled relentlessly, and for a fleeting moment she considered abandoning the night entirely, retreating to the safety of familiar walls where judgment couldn't reach her.

But Charlie remained beside her solid, unyielding. With an effortless flourish, he opened the door.

The room exploded into colour and life.

Laughter and chatter washed over her as if she'd stepped into another world. Golds, emeralds, and deep ruby hues shimmered throughout the space, weaving together like a tapestry pulled from a faraway land. The air was rich with warm spices and promise, alive with movement and joy. What had once been an ordinary space now felt enchanted?

Everywhere she looked, people laughed freely, their happiness infectious. Ellie and Lily drifted through the crowd like animated butterflies, their energy unmistakable. Hope flickered in Sara's chest fragile, but real. *Maybe this could be okay,* she thought. *Maybe I can do this but* then her gaze snagged. Victoria stood nearby, flawless hair, radiant smile, glowing effortlessly beside her boyfriend. The familiar sting of comparison struck instantly. Panic surged, memories of inadequacy tightening around her chest.

No, I can't do this.

Her heart raced as she teetered on the edge of escape once more. But before fear could take hold, Charlie gently redirected her attention.

Sara's father stood a short distance away, engrossed in conversation with his remarkably young girlfriend a pairing that felt conspicuous, like a mismatched puzzle piece forced into place. The sight extinguished what little elation Sara had managed to summon, replacing it with a fresh surge of discomfort and the looming certainty of awkward exchanges she wasn't sure she was ready for.

"Come on," Charlie urged gently, his voice steady and resolute as he squeezed her hand.

"We're going to face this head-on."

Anchored by his calm, they moved towards the group. Charlie extended a firm handshake to her father, the two men sizing each other up in a silent, unspoken standoff, polite, controlled, yet charged with tension that crackled like a live wire between them.

"Well then," Charlie said lightly, clapping his hands together, "what's everyone's bet?"

The question cut cleanly through the silence.

He smiled as if inviting mischief, determined to untangle the web of nerves tightening around them all.

Sara's father raised an eyebrow, curiosity flickering across his face as glances darted around the small circle. The heaviness began to loosen, just slightly, as Charlie pressed on.

"Let's make it interesting," he added, his tone playful now.

"Which of us has the greatest age difference between our partners?"

Then laughter bubbled up. hesitant at first, then freer, lifting the weight that had settled so heavily over the moment. Sara's father cast a sideways look at his girlfriend, uncertainty giving way to reluctant amusement as smiles spread through the group. The tension lingered for only a heartbeat longer before Sara burst into laughter, bright and genuine. Her joy was contagious, and soon others joined in, the atmosphere softening into something warm and human.

Relief flooded her chest.

Gratitude followed swiftly for Charlie, for his maturity, his instinctive kindness, and his ability to disarm even the most fragile moments with grace and humour. He had steered the evening onto As Sara prepared to excuse herself and wander towards the dazzling array of clothes on display, a sudden sensation stopped her short.

A gentle kick. Then another.

Her breath caught as delight exploded through her, banishing the remnants of anxiety in an instant. It was strange and wonderful and impossibly real, a reminder of the tiny life growing within her, grounding her completely in the moment.

"Oh!" she laughed, pressing a hand to her belly.

"The baby, he's kicking! Who wants to feel?"

Her excitement rippled outward, igniting a burst of delighted chaos as eyes widened and voices overlapped. The group instinctively leaned closer, curiosity and wonder drawing them in. Hands hovered, tentative and eager, as laughter filled the space once more.

The awe was unmistakable quiet and shared.

Victoria, ever confident and animated, stepped in with her usual sparkle, ushering everyone forward and encouraging them on, transforming the moment into something joyous and communal. A celebration of life unfolding in real time.

"Charlie, you should go first."

At those words, something profound settled in Sara's chest. Her heart swelled, emotion rushing through her like a tide. It felt like a quiet blessing, an unspoken acknowledgement that her mother saw Charlie not as a complication, but as someone capable of being a good father, a steady partner, a presence worthy of trust.

Charlie knelt carefully, reverently, and placed his hand against her belly. When the baby kicked again, unmistakable this time, they both froze, breath caught in tandem. The moment was small, fleeting… and yet impossibly significant. It tethered them together in a way words never could, wrapping the space between them in something tender and sacred.

Laughter and warmth reigned among her friends and family, chasing away earlier shadows of doubt and fear.

Conversations sparked effortlessly, light-hearted stories overlapping as joy stitched itself into the evening. Each voice, each smile, added another thread to a tapestry of connection that felt newly strengthened.

For the first time that night, Sara felt she could truly breathe.

This wasn't just about confronting anxiety anymore. It was about celebrating beginnings. About stepping into uncertainty with support at her back and love at her side. The music swelled, vibrant and infectious, transforming the room into something alive. A celebration pulsing with promise.

Sara's heart, beat in time with it all. Each rhythm echoing resilience, hope, and the quiet thrill of what lay ahead. Laughter danced through the air like pixie dust, and she realised she was ready to embrace the unknown, to trust joy again, to let herself believe.

With Charlie standing beside her, grounded and unwavering, she felt stronger. Braver. Excited for the chapters still waiting to unfold.

She guided his hand more firmly against her stomach, love surging through her veins.

Charlie's eyes lit up as he felt the movement again.

Sara's vision blurred, emotion softening everything around her.

Then Charlie lifted his head, a sudden thought striking him.

"Wait," he said slowly. "Did you say *he*?"

CHAPTER 32: Ellie

To call the *Dubai Nights* party at Shoperapy a success would have been an understatement. It may well have been the best night of Ellie's life a night where magic lingered in the air, blending effortlessly with laughter, love, and long-held dreams finally given room to breathe. As the evening began to wind down, Ellie paused to take it all in.

Her shop glowed.

Thanks to Lily and Amir's tireless efforts, Shoperapy had been transformed into something otherworldly. Vibrant banners swayed gently from the ceiling, fairy lights coiled around shelves like constellations brought down to earth, and every corner shimmered with warmth. The space felt alive not just decorated but *celebrated*. Pride swelled in Ellie's chest as she realised, not for the first time, just how much she had built from the ground up.

The shop brimmed with wonderful women, most accompanied by the people they loved. Stories overlapped, laughter rose and fell, and joy sparked through the room like fireworks against a velvet sky. As Ellie drifted between conversations, she felt a profound sense of belonging. This wasn't just a party; it was proof of the community she had nurtured. A chosen family stitched together by encouragement, resilience, and shared moments that had coloured their lives with hope.

Across the room, she spotted Sara and Charlie.

They stood close, their smiles glowing softly in the dim light. Sara radiated a quiet, expectant warmth, the gentle beauty of someone standing at the edge of a new beginning. Ellie knew their story well. Though Charlie wasn't the baby's biological father, his devotion was unmistakable. She watched him rub Sara's back absentmindedly, murmuring reassurance, anchoring her with tenderness and calm. Sara looked safe. Loved.

Nearby, Victoria lingered once wary, now smiling. The shift was subtle but unmistakable. Acceptance had settled in, reshaping old doubts into understanding. Ellie felt a quiet satisfaction bloom at the sight. Family, she thought, wasn't always about blood. Sometimes it was about choice, presence, and love shown through action.

Not far away, Lily stood slightly apart from the crowd, a sparkling drink cradled in her hand. Her gaze wandered, thoughtful, her brow faintly furrowed as she wrestled with her feelings for Teddy. Watching her, Ellie was transported back to the moment Lily had chosen to leap, to leave behind the only city she'd ever known and a job that had been safe, predictable, and quietly stifling. It hadn't been an easy decision, but it had been the right one.

"You're doing this, Lil," Ellie had told her earlier that evening.

"Face it head-on. You'll be alright."

Seeing Lily now standing in uncertainty yet refusing to retreat, filled Ellie with pride. Courage didn't always roar. Sometimes it simply stayed.

Then the door opened again.

Chase entered with Ryan, not as his boss, but as his date. The energy between them was unmistakable, bright, and electric, rippling through the shop. Ellie smiled as she watched them laugh together, warmth settling deep in her chest. She knew Chase had been annoyed when she'd accidentally revealed his feelings a secret spilled too soon but the result stood right in front of her now. A genuine smile. A risk rewarded.

Ellie exhaled softly, heart full.

Shoperapy hummed with love in all its forms bold, fragile, unexpected, and brave. And standing there amid the glow, Ellie realised something quietly extraordinary:

This wasn't just a chapter closing. It was a beginning.

Seeing him so happy made Ellie chuckle softly as she thought, *if my little slip led to that kind of joy for him, I suppose I'll be pushing his buttons for the rest of my life.* The idea filled her with warmth and quiet amusement.

The atmosphere inside Shoperapy felt buoyant, lifted by happiness echoing from every corner. Just when Ellie thought the night couldn't possibly improve, the door opened once more.

Amy and Noah stepped inside.

Ellie recognised them instantly and nearly gasped. They were arm in arm, laughing freely, utterly absorbed in one another as though the rest of the world had dissolved around them. They moved through the shop wrapped in their own bubble of joy, drawing curious glances and quiet smiles from everyone they passed.

Amy floated by Ellie, glowing, eyes sparkling, offering only a distracted, dreamy,

"Hello," before disappearing deeper into the shop. Ellie followed her with her gaze then did a double take.

Wait… was that spray paint on Amy's cheek?

Bright flecks of colour dusted her skin. chaotic, playful, oddly charming. The sight made Ellie smile, nostalgia tugging gently at her chest as she remembered carefree days of messy creativity, laughter, and not worrying about consequences.

Amy and Noah drifted towards Jess and Adam, their laughter ringing through the air like music. Ellie watched as the four of them fell easily into conversation, smiles wide, energy warm and magnetic. Something unmistakable was forming there, not just romance, but connection. A new branch of family growing in real time, rooted in friendship and shared joy.

It filled Ellie with a deep, contented warmth.

Overwhelmed by the moment, she crossed the room to Lily, who was quietly observing it all, a soft smile playing on her lips, eyes shining with calm acceptance.

"Can you believe this? It's like a scene from a movie," Ellie said, her voice infused with delight and disbelief. Lily turned, her eyes sparkling with excitement,

Lily turned to her, excitement dancing in her gaze.

"Honestly? It's better than anything I imagined. Just look at them."

They stood together for a moment, soaking it all in.

Snippets of conversation floated through the hum of Shoperapy. Sara animatedly debated nursery colours with Charlie including soft yellows, gentle greens. Her hands moving as fast as her imagination.

Nearby, Chase was mid-story, dramatically recounting a recent escapade with Ryan, his enthusiasm contagious. Ryan, never one to be outdone, launched into a tale of his own, arms flapping as he spoke.

"And then I slipped in the mud," he said, eyes wide with theatrical flair, "but instead of falling sideways, I just plopped straight back like a penguin!"

The group erupted into laughter, the sound spilling across the room and weaving itself into the magic of the night. The joyous atmosphere wrapped around Ellie like a warm embrace as memories were forged beneath the lights. A living reminder that they were all here, together, sharing something rare and fleeting.

Gratitude swelled in her chest as she took in the vibrant life unfolding around her. Moments like this didn't come often, and when they did, they carried a weight of meaning that lingered long after the night ended.

Stepping back, Ellie slipped into a quiet corner, allowing herself a moment to breathe it all in. She wanted to capture this feeling, to anchor it somewhere deep within her gratitude not only for what the night had become, but for the community she had built through passion, perseverance, and an unwavering belief in empowering women.

There was magic in the air now. a sense that something meaningful had been born. She saw it in the way conversations deepened, in how laughter flowed freely and connections formed beyond polite acquaintance. This was what she had envisioned amidst the daily chaos: a tapestry woven from resilience, joy, and friendship.

"Let's toast, everyone!"

Ellie's voice cut through the hum of conversation as she raised her glass. Laughter softened, heads turned, anticipation rippling through the room.

"To new beginnings, and the stories we create together."

Applause erupted, vibrant and heartfelt, glasses clinking in joyful unison. Ellie's heart swelled as realisation settled in, she was part of something extraordinary. They were no longer just individuals sharing a space… they were a circle, a chosen family bound together by Shoperapy.

As the music got louder, Ellie allowed herself to be carried by the rhythm of the evening. What had begun as a party had transformed into a celebration of life, love, and human connection. Challenges would come. Shadows always followed light, but tonight, they were cocooned in warmth and laughter. Together, they would face whatever lay ahead. Together, they were unstoppable.

Amir appeared at her side, offering a drink a vibrant cocktail garnished with lime and delicate rose petals, a nod to Dubai's golden elegance.

The gesture stirred something tender in her chest. He wasn't just handsome; he was thoughtful, kind, his smile as warm as the evening air.

Standing near the edge, Ellie gazed out across the city, the last traces of autumn warmth brushing her skin. For a fleeting moment, she could almost picture a beautiful life with him.

"Amir," she said softly, barely audible above the distant hum of the streets.

"Can we talk?"

He nodded, his dark eyes searching hers, already sensing the truth. The sun dipped low over the ocean, casting gold across the skyline breathtaking, bittersweet.

"You've decided then," he said quietly.

Ellie swallowed, the weight in her chest growing heavier.

"I can't let this go," she replied, emotion threading through her voice.

"Shoperapy. The women. The future of this community. It's my life now."

Understanding flickered in Amir's eyes, not surprise, but acceptance.

"I'm sorry," Ellie added. "Truly, Amir."

He leaned in, pressing a gentle kiss to her cheek, a silent gesture of support, of respect.

He understood. Of course he did.

CHAPTER 33: Lily

Lily approached the meeting point where she was due to meet her private tour guide.

Who? Teddy, of course.

She knew exactly who she was meeting he didn't.

Booking under a different name had felt safer. Using her real one had filled her with dread. Teddy had been hurt, and she feared he wouldn't even show if he knew it was her. Ghosting him for days had been easier than facing the truth or the possibility that she'd broken something beyond repair.

As she drew closer, butterflies erupted in her stomach, a volatile mix of excitement and fear. Each step pulled memories to the surface: laughter, shared secrets, long walks through this very town. What had once felt magical now carried the weight of unfinished business. Her heart thudded painfully as questions crowded her mind.

What if he refused to talk?

What if he walked away?

When Teddy finally turned and saw her, the shift in his expression was immediate. Disappointment flickered across his handsome features, quickly followed by hurt, sharp and unmistakable. The chill in his eyes sent a shiver through her.

She swallowed hard, resisting the urge to turn and run.

"Look, Lily," he said, his voice tight, distant, even more formal than she remembered.

"I can't talk right now. I've got a private tour booked. The guest should be here any minute."

Hearing her name spoken aloud made her pulse spike.

"Is it with Ms. Ana Asif?" she asked, her voice a mixture of determination and uncertainty.

Teddy's brow furrowed in confusion, a slight blush creeping across his cheeks.

"Well, yes... but how did you"

Realisation struck. His posture shifted as he folded his arms across his chest, a defensive wall snapping into place, one she recognised all too well.

Lily didn't hesitate.

"Asif means 'sorry' in Arabic," she said softly, a tentative smile tugging at her lips.

"Right," he said, still not entirely convinced.

"Well, you paid for the tour, so I'll give you what you paid for. Just follow me."

Without waiting for a response, Teddy turned and started walking. His shoulders seemed heavier than usual, his steps edged with sulkiness that made Lily's chest tighten.

After a few paces, she slowed, her courage wavering. *What am I doing?*

Her hand twitched at her side, aching to reach for his, to close the distance she'd created.

"Actually..." she said quietly.

Teddy stopped. He turned, his eyebrows lifting in surprise.

"Well," he shrugged, a hint of curiosity slipping through his reluctance.

"It *is* your money. I suppose we can do whatever you want." Lily replied.

"Oh, I think we should continue with the tour." Teddy grinned.

It wasn't quite forgiveness, but it was something. A crack in the ice. A fragile spark of hope.

As they walked on together, Lily noticed the familiar charm lingering beneath his guarded exterior. His smile still surfaced now and then, reluctant but real. She felt it the truth she'd been afraid to name.

He still cared.

Beneath the frost, warmth remained.

They walked through the town together, a comfortable silence settling between them. It wasn't empty, it was heavy with things left unsaid, threaded with shared memories that lingered in every street they passed. Old laughter echoed in Lily's mind, colliding with the weight of everything she hadn't yet explained.

She stopped abruptly outside an unremarkable building.

"Here we are."

Teddy glanced up, unimpressed.

"This place isn't anything special," he said. "Just another apartment building."

He folded his arms, boredom flickering across his face — unaware that this was no ordinary stop, but the quiet unveiling of a future she'd been too afraid to admit out loud. Lily felt anticipation flutter deep in her chest.

"Ah," she replied, a knowing smile playing on her lips,

"But you're forgetting something."

She straightened slightly.

"I'm the tour guide now, remember? And this place is *especially important*."

Teddy watched her cautiously as she continued, her excitement bubbling over.

"This is where I've rented an apartment," she announced brightly.

"All right. next stop!"

She turned and started walking again.

For a moment, Teddy didn't move.

Then, "Wait. Did you just say?"

"Please," Lily interrupted, lifting a hand in mock seriousness,

"No questions until the end of the tour."

Her grin was playful, but her heart pounded as she whisked him along, hope and nerves tangling with every step.

Their next stop was a small artist's studio tucked away on a quiet street. Sunlight poured through tall windows, illuminating splashes of colour, fabrics draped over tables, sketches pinned haphazardly to the walls, half-formed ideas waiting to come alive. It was chaotic. Alive. Entirely hers.

"This," Lily said, gesturing animatedly, "It's going to be my creative haven." She spun slowly, arms wide.

"I'll make my scarves here. Each one will tell a story of nostalgia, humour, little moments stitched into fabric. No two will ever be the same."

Teddy stared at her, momentarily speechless. Her passion softened something in him, drawing a reluctant smile to his lips despite his lingering confusion.

Next, she led him to Shoperapy the boutique buzzing with life even after hours.

"Imagine it," she said, eyes alight.

"Colours everywhere. Laughter. Customers becoming friends. A few fashion disasters along the way."

"Sounds like chaos," Teddy said dryly.

She laughed.

"The good kind."

That small exchange, that easy banter, felt like a crack in the wall between them. Tiny, but real.

Then she brought him to their old Italian restaurant, just down the street. The scent of garlic and warm bread drifted through the doorway, tugging memories to the surface.

"This is where we'll have dinner every Friday," Lily said softly.

"Too much pasta. Too much wine."

Teddy raised an eyebrow, memories flickering behind his guarded gaze.

"And here," she continued, pointing towards the cinema nearby, "movie nights. Rom-coms we pretend not to love. Thrillers where you steal my popcorn."

She smiled as she gestured to the marquee glowing above them.

Reaching into her bag, Lily held up two tickets.

"Next Wednesday."

She looked at him then really looked, her breath caught somewhere between hope and fear.

The tour wasn't just about places. It was an invitation.

"It will be our first outing as partners in crime," Lily said triumphantly,

"My creations and your charm."

Teddy shook his head again, but this time a genuine half-smile surfaced, the last traces of ice beginning to melt.

"Think I can survive the blatant commercialism?" he asked, his voice noticeably lighter.

It felt different now, like they were finally sharing the same moment instead of standing on opposite sides of it. A small shift, but a meaningful one.

With every stop, Lily revealed more than locations. She revealed intention. Each place carried a story, a memory, or a dream, all carefully stitched together like the scarves she longed to create. Slowly, the tension Teddy had carried began to loosen its grip. His humour returned in fragments, his confusion still present but softened by curiosity.

What had started as an awkward encounter was quietly transforming into something hopeful.

After an animated exchange about scarf patterns and colours, Lily turned to him, mischief dancing in her eyes.

"So," she said lightly, "ready for one last surprise?"

Teddy sighed dramatically.

"Do I even have a choice?"

"Not really!" she chirped, already leading the way.

Their final stop was a small park tucked away from the noise of the city a place that held stolen ice creams, late-night conversations, and whispered secrets beneath star-filled skies.

Teddy slowed as they reached it, disbelief softening into recognition.

"So… this is where the grand tour ends?"

"Yes!" Lily said, beaming as she gestured around them.

"This is the real value. The place where memories are made. For a fleeting second, Teddy's eyes glistened. Something unguarded flickered there understanding, warmth, acceptance.

"Lily," he said quietly,

"I have to admit… this has been the most unexpected tour of my life."

She stepped closer, her heart pounding but hopeful.

At that moment, she knew the storm brewing between them was starting to ease. She smiled, stepping forward, hopeful and tentative.

"And you didn't even have to pay too much for this one."

He chuckled, shaking his head.

"Well, I suppose every misadventure has a silver lining."

Their eyes held. The weight of everything unspoken lingered between them, but it no longer felt heavy, just unfinished.

Finally, Teddy broke the silence, grinning.

"I'm sorry," he said, "but I have a particularly important question. One I really need answered."

Lily smiled. "Alright. Go on."

He leaned in slightly, excitement barely contained.

"Is this your way of telling me… that you're staying?"

Her smile softened.

"And how would you feel if I said it was?"

Teddy didn't answer with words.

He leaned in and kissed her gently at first, then with certainty, the kind of kiss that spoke of relief, forgiveness, and something choosing to begin again.

Later that night, before sleep found him, Teddy had one more thing to do, and one person to thank for the day that had changed everything.

And he knew exactly how to do it.

REVIEW OF SHOPERAPY

Teddy - Meadowbank Tour Guide...

In the heart of the town, Shoperapy dazzles fashion enthusiasts. With its warm hues and soft lighting, the boutique lures shoppers in. Ellie, the creative owner, offers not only fashion guidance but advice on friendship and love. Fresh flowers scent the air, creating a serene shopping retreat. Shoppers leave with not only a new outfit but confidence, making Shoperapy a cherished destination for all. **You definitely need to visit, or why not book one of my tours, as I'll be adding Shoperapy to my tour route as a must see highlight of Meadowbank for all you shoppers.**

CHAPTER 34: Ellie

Ellie and Amir filled the final days of his visit with laughter, quiet conversations, and far too many overpriced Matchas and cakes. But now, as the sun sank beneath the horizon bleeding peach and violet across the sky their borrowed time was drawing to a close.

The hotel room hummed softly as Ellie watched Amir pack. He lifted a pair of socks and a top from his suitcase and grinned.

"You can start your grand romantic gesture now."

Ellie laughed, the sound light and melodic. If this were a romantic comedy, she imagined swelling music, a dramatic declaration, and a mad dash to the airport. Instead, she found comfort in the stillness. In the ordinary. In the life she had built with intention. Shoperapy. The women. The community that felt like home.

The elevator doors slid shut with a gentle chime, sealing them into a small, suspended moment. Amir turned to her, mischief dancing in his eyes.

"Now?" he teased. "Is this when you do it?"

"Are you going to do your grand gesture now?" His wink had the impeccable timing of a seasoned comedian, causing her cheeks to flush despite herself.

Her cheeks warmed. Words crowded her mind every noun, every verb scrambling for attention but the sentence that mattered most refused to form. The elevator descended. So did the moment.

At the airport, tension hung thick in the air as Amir checked in. When the attendant asked if they were travelling together, Amir's eyebrow lifted, hope flickering across his face.

Ellie smiled softly and shook her head.

"You really missed your moment just then," Amir said later, amused rather than bitter.

"That would've been perfect."

"That would have been the perfect time for your grand romantic gesture."

Ellie attempted to suppress a giggle, feeling the warmth of both embarrassment and delight rise within her. It was a soft ending to an amazing week, one that filled her heart, yet left her teetering on the edge of a decision.

As they prepared to part ways, Amir kept the flame of encouragement alive, giving her myriad opportunities to make her move. Their embrace hung in the air, thick with unexpressed emotions, until Amir stepped back, eyes glinting with a cheeky determination.

"It's not too late! You could still go buy a ticket!"

"Darling," Ellie called out, her heart dancing despite the distance growing between them,

"I have a ticket, darling! A golden one. Sorry, it just doesn't go to Dubai!"

He blew her kisses, disappearing into the throng of bustling travellers, while Ellie felt the wave of reality crash over her. Sighing, she thought of other blown chances at love and fallen opportunities slipping through her fingers like sand. Had she missed yet another cue meant just for her?

But perhaps that was the bittersweet nature of her heart; even always questioning, she understood that Amir had been the closest she had ever come to forever. And that was a treasure worth holding onto.

With a heavy heart, Ellie drove back to town, the landscape reflecting her inner turmoil. Every passing light on the road flickered like the thoughts racing through her mind. But upon arriving at Shoperapy, her worries began to lift. Almost as if a hug awaited her; as she stepped inside, the shop welcomed her like an old friend.

To her surprise, Grace arrived not for work, but to buy a perfect dress for her upcoming date with Everett. The air filled with giggles and fond discussions about love, as if the universe conspired to mend her heart with friendship.

Then Sara burst through the door excitedly, holding her latest ultrasound.

"Look, Ellie! I'm really having a baby!"

Her exuberance was contagious, lighting the dim corners of Ellie's heart.

And then came Amy and Noah, with a small stack of photos Ellie had not even realised they had taken. Noah, the artist, shared his latest project about how communities come together. They spoke, animated and enthusiastic, while Ellie flipped through the pictures. Her heart echoed warmth at the happiness of shared moments: there was the first time she met Amy, giggling over accidental brushstrokes of paint. The image of the girls camped out on a stakeout inside her shop, armed with snacks and what they'd optimistically called 'stakeout gear.'

Then a powerful reminder of the community meeting aimed at stopping a vandal, her head down, focusing with fierce determination as she emailed Amir, her heart held tightly by the threads of friendship.

And there was another, showing Jess and Amy bonding cheekily over spray-painting their ideas on the back of the shop, clearly none the wiser about what trouble they might be stirring up, and of course… the orange jumpsuits they would soon be wearing. A great antidote for the best man's speech.

Along with the photographs, Noah took out his phone and showed everyone an article that had been uploaded from the local newspaper about his 'Art.'

> **Meadowbank Express: Wednesday @9:25am**
> **The recent vandalising incidents in Meadowbank have taken an unexpected turn. What some labelled as vandalism was actually a community project created by up-and coming artist Noah Bradford. Noah said,**
> "This vibrant piece of art celebrates the heart of our community, emphasising the spirit of togetherness in Meadowbank and a little place we all know as Shoperapy."
> **Noah, who found inspiration in the everyday lives of the town's people, revealed, "I wanted to show how art can bring us together, not divide us." His expressive work displays images of friends and families joyfully engaging in Meadowbank illustrating how the town fosters connections.**
> **Residents are echoing this sentiment. Ellie, owner of Shoperapy remarked,**
> "It's not just paint on a wall; it's a representation of our community."
> Amy, another local, added,
> "I love that art can spark conversations and connectivity. Noah's work does just that!"
> **You can see Noah's artwork in his local exhibition at Community Hall.**

Ellie felt a revitalising bliss wrap around her. Perhaps her recent heartache was not the end of love but instead an intoxicating reminder of feelings that were fleeting yet heartfelt. Here, while sharing happiness, she rediscovered that it was the laughter, the connections and relationships that filled her heart with happiness.

Returning her gaze to the scene unfolding before her, she embraced the reality that love was multifaceted. Though Amir was now thousands of miles away, the bonds she had nurtured with her friends anchored her. They were a fortifying network against loneliness. Each snapshot of laughter and support whispered that she was never truly alone. Each memory felt like the brushstrokes in Noah's art, joining together to form a portrait of a life rich with love and friendship.

Smiling, she put down the photographs, looking around the space filled with familiarity. A chapter may have ended, but a new one would begin with each day. Maybe tomorrow wouldn't come with grand gestures of love, but it could still be filled with simple moments of happiness. That was a dreamy reality she was entirely happy to live in.

Ellie thought as she observed the scene in front of her… this was the perfect remedy for heartbreak: allowing yourself to feel the emotion and remember the good times, surround yourself with amazing friends and do what you love…. which for Ellie, was continuing to create the community of friendships at Shoperapy.

Love would come later, she thought, once she was done once more forswearing it for good!

Blog:
Posted: 11:55 PM (GMT)
User: Your Fashion Ellie-vator
Subscribers: 987

Hello, you Gooooooorgeous fabulous friends! I can say that now, can't I? Tonight, I find myself reflecting on all that has transpired over the past few months here at Shoperapy. My heart is full as I think of my incredible friends and the amazing adventures they are embarking on. Each of their stories is interwoven with my own, creating shared experiences that I cherish dearly.

First and foremost, I've learned so much about myself, my shop, and the wonderful community that surrounds us. In the process of helping others find the perfect outfits, I've also unearthed some profound insights about my own desires and needs. Love, with all its beauty, can complicate things so easily, leading to heartache and uncertainty. With these thoughts swirling inside me, I've made a firm commitment to keep my heart safe for now... would-be boyfriends, take heed, I'm giving up on romance once again.

On a brighter note, the most joyous news is that Jess and Adam are taking their relationship to the next level! With Amy's enthusiastic approval, the wedding plans are already in full swing, and the excitement is contagious. I can hardly contain my enthusiasm for them as they plan this beautiful chapter of their lives together, and I feel so privileged to be part of their love story.

Speaking of love, Chase has truly blossomed and is absolutely head over heels for Ryan. Witnessing their budding romance makes me so happy, and I can only hope that they continue nurturing what they have; their joy is infectious, and it makes me believe in love just a little bit more.

In a turn of events that can only be described as miraculous, Sara has finally received her parents' blessing for her relationship with Charlie. Their approval was something Sara longed for, and I'm thrilled that she can now share her happiness openly, without reservation. The joy on her face when she told us the news was utterly heartwarming and a testament to the power of love and understanding. Each of these developments has reminded me of the value of friendship and support, reinforcing the fact that we are all in this together.

On the work front, Amy is keeping busy too, helping Noah prepare for his upcoming exhibition. I wholeheartedly encourage everyone to attend. It promises to be an inspiring event that you won't want to miss.

So, what's coming up next in Shoperapy?

Well, in true Ellie fashion, I can't seem to sit still. Yes, you've guessed it… I will be dressing Jess and her bridal party for her wedding! Oh my, wedding guest dresses are a whole new ballgame for me, and I don't want to let Jess down. The thought of looking for beautiful, bespoke gowns for her special day fills me with both excitement and a touch of anxiety, but I'm ready to take on this challenge with every piece of my heart and I do have Lily and Grace's creative minds to help me.

Remember, please keep visiting Shoperapy! I can't wait to see each of you soon for some retail therapy and hear about your own mishaps, loves, and dreams.

So, with a mix of excitement and determination, I'll dive into these new challenges headfirst.

Love always, Ellie xx

Acknowledgements

Again, the swirl of emotions overwhelms me as I finish my second book. Heartfelt thanks to every reader, reviewer, and supporter of Shoperapy; your kindness fuels my passion.

To my family and friends, again I owe you all a debt of gratitude. Your amazing love and support give me the encouragement that allows me to continue to pursue my dream. Your presence in my life has provided me with countless experiences worth writing about, from stories of family and friendship over the years to the countless mishaps and all things fabulous.

To my editor, Sarah, I owe you my journey of not one but four books. With each book, your encouragement transforms my fears into novels, and I look forward to continuing my journey with you as I complete the Shoperapy series.

Lastly, to the amazing females whose lives continue to intersect with mine, thank you for the laughter, love, and everything in between. Thank you so much for continuing to be my muse.

I hope the pages read reflects the friendship, love, and laughter you have all showered upon me and inspire others in their own journeys, to dream big!

Love Stephanie xxx

About the Author

Stephanie Scott lives in Scotland and is married with four gorgeous adult children. She is a Depute Head Teacher and has worked in Education for almost 30 years. Her passion has always been writing since she could hold a pen. It has always been her dream to write a fun series that women could relate to.

She loves all things fabulous: family, friendships, fashion, and fun.

You can connect with me on:
Instagram @stephaniescott_author
Email: stephaniescottauthor70@gmail.com

www.ingramcontent.com/pod-product-compliance
Ingram Content Group UK Ltd.
Pitfield, Milton Keynes, MK11 3LW, UK
UKHW021319110326
11208UKWH00008B/1407